THE
WEDDING
CHARADE

THE WEDDING CHARADE

BY

MELANIE MILBURNE

First published in Great Britain 2011
by Mills & Boon, an imprint of Harlequin (UK) Limited,
Large Print edition 2011
Eton House, 18-24 Paradise Road,
Richmond, Surrey TW9 1SR

© Melanie Milburne 2011

ISBN: 978 0 263 22202 9

Harlequin (UK) policy is to use papers that are natural,
renewable and recyclable products and made from
wood grown in sustainable forests. The logging and
manufacturing process conform to the legal environmental
regulations of the country of origin.

Printed and bound in Great Britain
by CPI Antony Rowe, Chippenham, Wiltshire

To Georgina (Georgie) Brooks:
a friend, a fan and a fabulous young woman.
This one is for you! XX

CHAPTER ONE

'THERE'S a Jade Sommerville here to see you, Signor Sabbatini,' Nic's secretary, Gina, informed him as she brought in his morning coffee. 'She said she's not going to leave the building until you agree to speak to her.'

Nic continued to look through the prime real estate properties listed on his computer screen. 'Tell her to make an appointment like everyone else,' he said, smiling to himself as he thought of Jade pacing the floor in Reception. It was just the sort of thing she would do: fly in to Rome on an impulse, demand her way no matter what, throwing her light weight around as if she had an inborn right to everything she wanted right when she wanted it.

'I think she really means it,' Gina said. 'In fact, I think—'

The door opened with a thud as it banged against the wall. 'Please leave us, Gina,' Jade said with a plastic-looking smile. 'Nic and I have some private business to discuss.'

Gina looked worriedly at Nic. 'It's all right, Gina,' he said. 'This won't take long. Hold my calls and make sure we are not interrupted under any circumstances.'

'Sì, Signor Sabbatini,' Gina said and left, closing the door with a soft click behind her.

Nic leaned back in his chair and surveyed the black-haired virago in front of him. Her green eyes were flashing with sparks of fury, the normally alabaster skin of her cheeks cherry-red. Her small hands were clenched into tight fists by her sides and her breasts—which he had secretly admired ever since she was sixteen—were heaving with every enraged breath she took. 'So, what brings you to my neck of the woods, Jade?' he asked with an indolent smile.

Her cat's eyes narrowed. 'You bastard!' she spat. 'I bet you put him up to it, didn't you? It's just the sort of underhand thing you would do.'

Nic raised a brow. 'I have no idea what you are talking about. Put whom up to what?'

She came over to stand in front of his desk, her hands slamming down on the leather top as she eyeballed him. 'My father is stopping my allowance,' she said. 'He's dissolved my trust fund. He's not giving me another penny. And it's all your fault.'

Nic allowed himself the luxury of the delectable view for a moment. Jade's creamy cleavage was about as close as it had ever been, apart from the night of her sixteenth birthday party. His nostrils flared as he caught a waft of the exotic fragrance she was wearing. It was an intriguing combination of jasmine and orange blossom and something else he couldn't put a name to, but it definitely suited her. He brought his gaze back to the fireworks show in hers. 'I might be guilty of many sins, Jade, but that is not one you can pin on me,' he said. 'I haven't spoken to your father in years.'

'I don't believe you,' she said, straightening from the desk.

She folded her arms across her body but if anything it gave him an even better view of those gorgeous breasts. He felt a stirring in his groin, the same rush of blood he always felt when around her. It annoyed him more than anything. He wasn't opposed to the odd one-night stand, but something about Jade made him wary of bedding her even for the short time it would take to do the deed. She oozed sensuality, but then she was known for her sleep-around ways. Only recently there had been a report in the press about her scandalous behaviour. She had allegedly lured a married man away from his wife and young family. Nic wondered how many men had enjoyed the experience of possessing her—or had *she* possessed them? She was a witch, after all: a little she-devil who liked nothing more than a full-on scene.

'Well?' she said, unfolding her arms and planting them on her slim hips in a combative manner. 'Aren't you going to say something?'

Nic picked up a gold pen off his desk and

clicked it a couple of times. 'What do you want me to say?'

She blew out a breath of fury. 'Are you deliberately being obtuse? You know what we have to do. You've known it for months and months. Now we've only got one month to make up our minds, otherwise the money will be lost.'

Nic felt an all too familiar spanner of anger tighten each vertebrae of his spine at the way his late grandfather had written his will. He had spent the last few months looking for a way out of it. He had consulted legal experts but to no avail. The old man's will was iron-clad. If Nic didn't marry Jade Sommerville by May the first, a third of the Sabbatini assets would be gone for ever. But a month was a month and he wasn't going to allow Jade to manipulate him into doing things her way. If he had to marry her—and it was very likely he would—he would do so on his terms and his terms only.

'So,' he said, drawling the word out as he swung his chair from side to side, his pen still clicking on-off, on-off. 'You want me to be your husband, do you, Jade?'

She glared at him like a wildcat. 'Technically, no,' she said. 'But I want that money. It was left to me and I don't care if I have to jump through hoops to get it, and no one can stop me.'

Nic smiled lazily. 'As far as I see it, *cara*, *I* am the one who can stop you.'

She strode back to the desk but, instead of standing in front of it, she came behind to where he was sitting. She grasped the top of the chair next to his left shoulder and swung him round to face her. She stood in between the intimate bracket of his open thighs, her warm vanilla-scented breath breezing over his face as she jabbed him in the chest with a French-manicured finger. Nic had never felt so turned on in his life.

'You. Will. Marry. Me. Nic Sabbatini.' She bit out each word as if she were spitting bullets.

He curled a lip as he held the green lightning of her gaze. 'Or else?' he said.

Her eyes flared, the thick black heavily mascara-coated lashes almost reaching her finely arched brows. She licked her mouth, making it glisten and shimmer, the action of her tongue sending a rocket-fuelled charge of blood to his pelvis.

Nic grabbed her hand before she could move away, wrapping his fingers around her wrist until they overlapped. 'You're going about this all wrong, Jade,' he said, pulling her farther in between his thighs. 'Why not use some of that sensual charm you're known for instead of coming at me like a cornered cat? Who knows what you might be able to talk me into doing, hmm?'

She flattened her mouth, her eyes full of disdain as they tussled with his. 'Let go of me,' she said through clenched teeth.

Nic elevated his eyebrow again. 'That's not what you were saying when you were sixteen.'

Her cheeks were like twin pools of crushed raspberries, which seemed strangely at odds with her cutting retort. 'You missed your chance, Italian boy. Your best friend took home the prize. He wasn't the best I've had but at least he was the first.'

Nic worked on controlling his breathing, dousing his blistering anger with the ice-cold water of common sense. She was deliberately goading him. It was what she did best. She had been doing it for as long as he had known her. She was a tart who used sex to get what she wanted.

He had done the honourable thing all those years ago, rejecting her advances, seeing them for what they were: a young, immature girl's grab for attention. He had lectured her about her behaviour but she had ignored his warning, deliberately seducing one of his closest friends to drive home her petulant point. It had destroyed his friendship with his mate and it had destroyed any respect he'd had for Jade. He had been prepared to give her a chance, but it seemed she was on the same path of destruction as her socialite mother had been before her death when Jade was a young child. 'You blame me for your father's withdrawal of your allowance, but don't you think it might have something to do with your recent affair with Richard McCormack?' he asked.

She tugged her wrist out of his hold and rubbed

at it pointedly. 'That was just a stitch-up in the press,' she said. 'He made a move on me but I wasn't interested.'

Nic gave a snort. 'It seems to me you're always interested. You're every man's fantasy. The wild-child party girl who will do anything to be the centre of attention.'

She gave him an arch look in return. 'You're a fine one calling me out for being a black kettle when your pot's been stirred by more women than any other man I know.'

Nic smiled at her imperiously because he knew it would inflame her. 'Yes, I know it's hypocritical of me, but there you have it. The double standard—even in spite of enlightened times—still exists. No man wants a tart for a wife.'

She frowned at him. 'So you're going to turn your back on your inheritance?'

He gave an indifferent shrug. 'It's just money.'

Her eyes widened again. 'But it's a fortune!'

'I'm already rich,' he said, enjoying the play of emotions on her face she was clearly struggling to disguise. 'I can earn double that in a couple of years if I put my mind to it.'

Her frown deepened. 'But what about your brothers? Won't Giorgio and Luca's shares in the Corporation be put in jeopardy if yours are given to an unknown third party?'

Nic schooled his features into a blank mask. 'If it happens, it happens. It's not what I would have wished but I can't compromise my standards to fit in with an old man's whimsical fantasy.'

This time she didn't bother trying to hide her outrage. 'But this is not just about you! It's about me as well. I need that money.'

Nic leaned back in his chair again and crossed his ankles. 'So go out and get a job,' he said. 'That's what other people who haven't been born into money do. You might even enjoy it. It will certainly make a change from having your nails and hair done.'

Her gaze seared his. 'I don't want a job,' she said. 'I want that money because your grandfather—my godfather—gave it to me. He wanted me to have it. He told me before he died that he would always be there for me.'

'I agree he wanted you to have the money,' Nic said. 'He had a rather soft spot for you. God knows why, given your track record of appalling behaviour, but he did. But he also wanted to manipulate me into doing things his way and that I will not stand for.'

She pressed her lips together as she swung away to pace the carpeted floor. Nic watched her from his chair. She was agitated and rightly so. Without her father's generous allowance, she was penniless. He knew for a fact she had no savings to speak of. She lived on credit and expected her father to clear it month by month. She had never had a job in her life. She hadn't even finished school. She had been expelled from three prestigious British fee-paying schools and then dropped out altogether a week after enrolment at the fourth. She was trouble with a capital *T*.

She turned back and came to stand in front of him again, her big green eyes taking on a soulful beseeching look. 'Please, Nic,' she said in a whisper-soft voice. 'Please do this one thing for me. I beg you.'

Nic drew in a long, slightly unsteady breath. She was bewitching and dangerous in this mood. He could feel the tentacles of temptation reaching out to ensnare him. He could feel the way his resolve was melting like wax under a blast of heat.

A year of marriage.

Twelve months of living together as husband and wife in order to secure a fortune. Thank God the press so far knew nothing about the terms of the will and Nic was determined to keep it that way. That would be the ultimate in public shame if word got out that he had been led to the altar with a noose around his neck, put there by his late grandfather.

But Jade was right. It was a fortune, and while he had every confidence he could earn it in his own right, given enough time, he was deeply worried about a third party shareholder. His brothers had been good about it so far. They had not put him under any undue pressure, but Nic knew

Giorgio, as the financial controller, was concerned given the ongoing economic instability across Europe.

Nic knew this was a chance to show his family and the press he was not the fool-around playboy everyone painted him as. He could make this one sacrifice to secure the Corporation's wealth and once the year was over he could get back to doing what he did best: being free from emotional entanglements. Being free to travel the world and take risks that others couldn't or wouldn't take. He thrived on it—the adrenalin and the surge of euphoric energy when a multimillion dollar deal was sealed.

He would agree to fulfil the terms of his grandfather's will but not because Jade told him to.

No one but no one told him what to do.

Nic pushed back the chair as he rose from it. 'I will have to get back to you on this,' he said. 'I have to go to Venice to check out a villa that's come on the market. I'll be away for a couple of days. I'll give you a call when I get back.'

She blinked up at him in bewilderment, as if

he had given the opposite answer to what she had been expecting. But then her beautiful face quickly reassembled itself into an expression of indignation. 'You're making me *wait* for your answer?' she asked.

Nic gave her a mocking smile. 'It's called delaying gratification, *cara*,' he said. 'Hasn't anyone told you if you wait a long time for something, when you finally get it the pleasure is a thousandfold?'

'I will make you pay for this, Nic Sabbatini,' she snarled. She stalked over to where she had dropped her designer handbag earlier and, scooping it up, flung the strap over one of her slim shoulders and gave him one last gelid glare before she left. 'You see if I don't.'

CHAPTER TWO

JADE arrived at the hotel in Venice at five in the afternoon. A member of the paparazzi had told her Nic was staying there, right on the Grand Canal. She was quite pleased with her detective work. Her sources had told her Nic was in a meeting until eight this evening, and then he would be returning to the hotel for a massage before a late dinner; she hadn't been able to find out if he was planning to dine alone or with one of his legion of female admirers.

Nic was the sort of man who had always had women swooning over him. She, to her eternal shame, had once been one of them. It still riled her that he had rejected her when she was sixteen and madly in love with him. Although she knew it was really her own fault for being so wilful, she couldn't help partly blaming him for the horrid experience of her first sexual encounter, not that she had ever told anyone. Even the man who had taken her virginity had no idea of how dreadful an ordeal it had been for her. But then she was good at deception. Deception was her middle name—well, it would be if she could spell it, she thought wryly.

She smiled at the concierge at the reception desk, fluttering her lashes in the manner she had perfected over the years. '*Scusi, signor.* I am meeting my fiancé here, Signor Nicolò Sabbatini. It is to be a very big… I don't know how to say it in Italian…a big surprise?'

The concierge smiled conspiratorially. '*Sì, signorina*, I understand—a *sorpresa.* But I did not know Signor Sabbatini was engaged. There has been nothing about it in the press, I am sure.'

There will be shortly, Jade thought with a mischievous private grin. '*Sì, signor*, it is all very hush-hush. You know how the Sabbatini brothers hate the intrusion of the press.' She pulled out a photo of her and Nic that had been taken at his grandfather's funeral. It wasn't a particularly intimate one but it showed Nic with his head leaning towards her as he whispered something before the service. Luckily, the shot didn't show her face for she had been scowling at him in fury at the time. Jade smiled at the concierge as she showed him the photograph. 'As you can see, we are never left alone by the press. That is why I wanted this to be our special time together before the world gets to know. I am so appreciative of your cooperation.'

'It is my pleasure, *signorina*,' he said and, handing back the photo, passed her a regulation form to fill in. 'If you would be so kind as to give your full name and address and country of residence for our records.'

Jade felt the familiar flutter of panic build in her chest. It was like a million micro bats' wings flapping all at once. She took a steadying breath and summoned up another megawatt smile. 'I am sorry, *signor*, but I have taken out my contact lenses for the flight,' she said. 'They are packed in my luggage somewhere. I am practically blind without them and I *hate* wearing glasses. So unfashionable, don't you think? Would you be so kind as to just type my details straight into your computer?'

The concierge smiled. 'But of course, *signorina*,' he said, his fingers poised over the keys as she gave him her details.

'You are so very kind,' Jade said as he handed her a swipe key.

'Signor Sabbatini is staying on the top floor in the penthouse suite. I will have your luggage taken to the room straight away.'

'*Grazie, signor.* But there is one more thing,' she said, leaning closer. 'Would you mind contacting the masseuse who was coming at eight?' She gave him a twinkling smile. 'I will give my fiancé a massage instead. He will enjoy it so much more, *sì*?'

The concierge grinned. '*Sì, signorina.* I am sure he will.'

Jade made her way to the lift, smiling at her reflection in the brass-plated doors once they were closed. She had dressed in her best look-at-me clothes. A black and sinfully short tight-fitting dress with a daringly low neck and shoes with the sort of heels podiatrists the world over shook their heads in dismay at, and flashy jewellery that screeched inherited wealth and decadence.

Jade found the room without any trouble and immediately ordered champagne. A bit of Dutch courage wouldn't go amiss right now. She would have to go carefully, however. She had to keep her wits about her in order to bring about what she wanted. Nic would be furious, but then that was his fault for being so stubborn about this. It was all right for him with his squillions, but what was she supposed to do without her trust fund? It wasn't as if she could just 'go out and get a job' as he had so mockingly suggested. Who on earth would employ her?

She looked out of the window to the bustling tourists below. The serpentine network of the canal system and the colourful villas fringing it was exactly as the postcards portrayed it. Even the light was the same: the pastels in the sky as the sun lowered brought out the pinks and oranges and yellows of the centuries-old buildings. She wished she had time to paint it. Her little makeshift studio back in her London flat was full to bursting with her work. Not that anyone had ever seen any of her paintings. It was her private passion. Something no one could rubbish, something no one could say was trashy and uneducated and unsophisticated.

Jade wandered over to the huge bed and tested it for comfort by pressing a hand down on the mattress. She snatched her hand away as she thought of all the women Nic had bedded on his trips. He would have lost count by now, surely? At least she could count her partners on the fingers of half a hand in spite of what the press reported of her sexual proclivities. Quite frankly, she wondered what the fuss about sex was all about. It didn't seem all that pleasurable to her to be pawed and sweated over. She could flirt and tease with the best of them and it got her what she wanted— well, most of the time.

The champagne arrived and Jade tipped the young man who brought it. She allowed herself one glass to settle her nerves. The time was dragging and she desperately wanted this to be over with so she could feel more secure. Nic had left her dangling, uncertain of whether he was going to cooperate or not. It was too risky to leave it all up to him. She had to force his hand, otherwise she would be destitute. She didn't mind pretending to be a tart at times but there was no way she was going to become one because all her other options had been destroyed.

Marrying Nic would solve everything for her. All her troubles would be over if she did what Salvatore's will stated. The lawyer had explained it all to her after the funeral last year. She had to marry Nic by the first of next month and stay married for a full year. Both partners had to remain faithful. Jade wasn't sure why her god-father had put that condition in. She didn't intend to sleep with Nic. He had spurned her in the past. What was to say he wouldn't do it again? She would find it just as shattering as she had then.

Jade was sipping at her second glass of champagne when Nic came in. His hazel eyes narrowed as he saw her sitting with her legs crossed on the bed. 'What the hell are you doing here?' he said.

'Celebrating our engagement,' she said with a demure smile as she hoisted her glass.

He stiffened as if he had been snap frozen. 'What did you say?' The words came out slowly, menacingly.

Jade took a sip from her glass, looking at him from beneath her lashes. 'The press already know about it,' she said. 'I gave them an exclusive. All they need now is a photo.'

Nic's anger was palpable. It rolled off the walls towards her, keeping her rooted to the foot of his bed. Jade fought the instinct to flee. She had been hit before. Her father had backhanded her for insolence enough times for her to know how much it hurt, but her pride would not let her show it. Instead, she gave Nic a defiantly sassy look. 'If you kick me out I will tell the press about the terms of your grandfather's will. You don't really want me to do that, do you, Nic?'

His top lip lifted in a snarl. 'You trashy, deceitful cow,' he said.

Jade let the words roll off her. 'Sticks and stones,' she said in a sing-song voice as she took another sip of champagne.

Nic strode over and snatched the glass out of her hand, spilling champagne over her lap in the process. She glared at him as she jumped up to wipe off the spillage. 'You bastard!' she said. 'This dress is brand new and now you've ruined it.'

His nostrils flared like those of an angry bull. 'Get out,' he said through tight lips. He pointed to the door with a rigid arm. 'Get out before I throw you out.'

Jade tossed her head and put her hand behind her back to unzip her damp dress. 'You put one finger on me and I'll tell even more Sabbatini secrets to the press.'

His mouth flattened to a thin line of fury. 'Do you have no principles at all?'

'Plenty,' she said, wriggling out of her dress.

His dark brows snapped together. 'What do you think you are doing?'

Jade tossed the dress on the floor, raising her

chin as she stood before him in black lace bra and knickers and her come-and-get-me heels. For a brief moment she wondered if she had stepped not just out of her dress but out of her depth as well. Nic's gaze seemed to be seeing through much more than her lacy underwear. She could feel the heat of it all over her skin, inside and out. She could feel a faint stirring deep inside her, a fluttering little pulse that seemed to intensify with each throbbing second. 'I'm going to have a bath,' she said, summoning her courage and resolve. 'Then, once I am freshened up, we are going out to publicly celebrate our engagement.'

He stood there, breathing heavily, his eyes hard on hers, hatred darkening them in a way she had never seen before. 'I am not letting you get away with this, Jade,' he warned. 'You don't get to screw around with me, do you hear?'

'What a lovely choice of words,' Jade said as she sashayed over to the bathroom. 'But there will be no screwing, OK? That's not part of the deal.' She gave him a saucy little fingertip wave and closed the bathroom door, clicking the lock firmly in place.

Nic let out a breath that felt as if it had come out of a steam engine. He was beyond angry. He was livid. He was furious.

He was screwed.

Jade had set him up and he had no choice but to go along with it. He would look a hundred times a fool if the press got wind of his grandfather's machinations. If he had to marry her, he would do it but he would make sure he didn't look like a pawn being pushed around.

He clenched and unclenched his fists. He wanted to knock that bathroom door down and drag that little scheming witch out by her long black hair. He had not thought it possible to hate someone so much. Was that what his grandfather had wanted? For him to hate the very air Jade Sommerville breathed? What had he been thinking to tie them together in a mock marriage for a whole year, for God's sake? It would be torture for him. Marriage to anyone would have been bad enough. He loathed the thought of being tied down to one person for any length of time, let alone the rest of his life.

Look what had happened to his father. He had not been able to remain faithful after the death of Nic's baby sister, and it had nearly destroyed his mother. Nic had been too young to remember Chiara, but he remembered the years that followed. Both his parents had been absent emotionally, cut to the core over the death of their precious daughter. Nic had run wild for most of his childhood, trying to get the assurances he needed as a young boy that he was still a much loved member of the family. But after losing one child, his parents had lived in fear of losing another and so they had held themselves aloof. Giorgio and Luca had fared better, being that bit older, but Nic knew he had missed out on what so many children took for granted.

Being forced to marry Jade was the worst possible scenario. For one thing, there was no way she would ever stay faithful for the allotted time. No wonder she was proposing a no sex deal. He wouldn't trust her as far as he could see her.

If he could guarantee she wouldn't stray, his inheritance would be secured. But the only way to ensure that would be to sleep with her, to make the marriage a real one. To keep her so satisfied she wouldn't be tempted to play around on him.

He rubbed at his jaw as he thought about it. Bedding Jade would certainly be an unforgettable experience. The blood was already fizzing in his veins from her brazen display of flesh. She had no shame, no limits at all on her behaviour. He smiled to himself as he thought about taking her in a rough tumble of lust. The sexual tension between them had crackled for as long as he could remember. It would certainly be no punishment for him to bury himself deep inside her, to make her scream his name instead of some nameless guy she had picked up in a nightclub.

Jade came out of the bathroom a long time later with her hair piled on top of her head and some damp tendrils hanging about her face. She was wearing one of the hotel's fluffy white bathrobes. Without her make-up and high heels, she looked young and dainty, her cheeks pink-skinned from her bath. As she moved past him to access her suitcase, Nic noticed she barely came up to his shoulder in her bare feet. Her toenails were painted black. They looked stark against the porcelain white of her skin.

'What happened to my massage appointment?' he asked.

She tucked a strand of hair behind one of her small ears without looking up from her open bag. 'I cancelled it.'

'You had no right to do that,' he said. 'I was looking forward to it.'

She glanced at him as she moved with a bundle of clothes to the wardrobe. 'I can give you one if you like,' she said. She hung a skirt and top on the silk-padded hangers. 'I'm told I'm very good.'

'I am sure you are,' Nic said, watching her move back to her bag.

She held up two dresses against her chest. 'Which one do you think?'

Nic had to give himself a mental shake. She was

doing it again: sideswiping him with her rapid change of demeanour. One minute the raging virago, the next a little girl playing at dress up. There would be another tantrum soon enough, he thought. 'The red one,' he said, striding over to the champagne sitting in the silver ice bucket. He poured himself a glass and sipped from it as he watched her dress.

She did it as if it were a strip show in reverse. She had slipped out of the bathrobe while he had been pouring his drink, but now she was stepping into a pair of black and red lacy French knickers that were gossamer-thin, so thin he could see the waxed clear feminine cleft of her body. His blood pounded all over again, making him uncomfortably stiff. He took another deep draught of champagne but he couldn't bear to drag his eyes away from her. She picked up a matching push-up bra. Not that she needed any mechanical help in showcasing her breasts. They were beautifully shaped, full and yet pert with rosy-red nipples. She adjusted the creamy globes behind the lace and then shook her head so her hair cascaded down over her back and shoulders.

Nic was fit to explode and he hadn't even touched her.

'Aren't you going to shower and change?' she said as she moved past him with her make-up bag.

He caught her arm on the way past, his fingers fizzing with the stun-gun effect of her warm flesh under his. He locked his eyes on her sea-glass green ones. 'How about that massage you promised?' he said.

She gave him a sultry look from beneath her lashes. 'Later,' she said. 'Dinner first. If you're a good boy I might give you a rub down when we get home.'

He tightened his hold when she made to pull away. 'Is this how you get every man to do what you want? To make them beg like starving dogs for your favours?'

She tossed her head again, making her hair swing back over her shoulders. 'You won't have to beg, Nic, because there will be no favours,' she said. 'This is going to be a paper marriage.'

Nic laughed out loud. 'Oh, come on, Jade. How long do you think that's going to last? You are a born sybarite.'

She glared at him as she tugged at his hold. 'I am not going to sleep with you.'

'Then what was the little tease routine for?' he asked.

She gave him a haughty look. 'You can look but you can't touch,' she said. 'That's the deal.'

Nic dropped her arm. 'There is something you need to learn about me, Jade,' he said. 'I choose my own sexual partners. I do the chasing. And I do not beg. Ever.'

She turned away and sat at the dressing table, opening various pots as she applied moisturiser and make-up. 'We'll see,' she said, meeting his eyes in the mirror.

Nic clenched his teeth and strode into the bathroom. *We'll see, indeed,* he thought as he turned on the shower full blast.

* * *

When Nic came out, Jade was sipping more champagne. She had her face on—the face he was used to seeing: heavy smoky eye-shadow and eyeliner, scarlet lipstick and a brush stroke of bronzing powder to highlight her model-like cheekbones. She was back in another pair of heels, even higher than the previous ones, and she had dangling earrings on that sparkled now and again behind the dark screen of her loose hair. She had a sulky look about her mouth, however, which warned him there might be another scene on its way.

He had thought through his options in the shower. He would marry her because he didn't really have a choice, but he would dictate the terms. She thought she had manipulated him into agreeing to it but he wasn't doing it for her, but for his family.

'Before we go to dinner I want to lay down some ground rules,' he said as he reached for a fresh shirt.

She crossed her legs and swung one high-heeled foot up and down in a bored schoolgirl manner.

'Go on then, tell me what they are and I'll tell you whether I'll agree to them or not.'

Nic whipped out a tie from the wardrobe. 'You will agree to it or I won't marry you. You're the one who needs the money more than me, don't forget.'

She set her mouth in a mulish line, her eyes hardening as she held his. 'So what are your stupid little rules, then?'

'I insist that at all times and in all places you will behave with the decorum your position as a Sabbatini wife requires of you,' he said. 'You have met both of my sisters-in-law, *sì*?'

'Yes, they are very nice,' she said. 'I met Bronte briefly at your grandfather's funeral. I met Maya, Giorgio's wife, in London. She had taken the time to call on me to show me the baby since I was unable to attend the christening. Matteo is adorable.'

'Yes, he is,' Nic said. 'So why didn't you come to the christening?'

Her eyes stayed determinedly away from his, her tone dismissive. 'I had another engagement.'

'And what about Luca and Bronte's son Marco's christening?' he asked. 'It was only a month later. Did you have another engagement that day too?'

This time she looked at him directly. 'I always keep myself busy. My social calendar is booked for months ahead.'

Nic felt his top lip curl. He could imagine her shoehorning in party after party, nightclub after nightclub, and shallow date after shallow date. 'It was good of you to come to my grandfather's funeral,' he said with no intention of it being a compliment. She had obviously known she was going to be included in the will, for why else would she have made the effort? He knew her well enough to know she didn't do anything for anyone unless she got something out of it for herself. 'You also came to see him before he died, didn't you?'

She nodded. 'It was the least I could do. He had always been so good to me. I was just his godchild. No one takes that role all that seriously these days, but he always looked out for me.'

'Apart from the will, of course,' Nic pointed out.

'Yes, well, he must have had his reasons.'

'Why do you think he did it?' Nic asked. 'To us, I mean. It's not as if we've been the best of friends over the years.'

She gave a little shrug of her slim shoulders. 'Who knows? Maybe he thought it would be a way of bringing the two dynasties together: the Sommervilles and the Sabbatinis. It has quite a ring to it. My father no longer has a male heir so this is the next best thing. I expect they cooked it up together.'

Nic studied her for a moment. 'You were supposed to be with your brother on that skiing holiday, weren't you?'

Her eyes shifted away from his. 'I missed the flight.' She gave a little shrug, as if it was just one of those things. 'I overslept after a night out.'

'Have you ever thought of how you could have both died if you had gone on that trip?' Nic asked. 'You would have been on the slopes with him when the avalanche hit.'

She gave him a glittering glare. 'Do you mind if we get back to your stupid little rules?'

'You don't like talking about Jonathan, do you?'

'You lost your baby sister,' she said. 'Do *you* like discussing it?'

'I don't even remember it,' he said. 'I was only eighteen months old. But Jonathan was twenty, almost twenty-one, and you were just weeks off turning eighteen. It must be very clear in your memory.'

'It is and it's off-limits,' she said, looking him in the eye. 'You might think you have certain privileges as my husband-to-be but that is not one of them.'

Nic pulled his tie up to his neck and straightened it, his eyes still following every nuance on her beautiful, now ice-maiden face. She could change so quickly it was amazing. 'The second rule is I will not tolerate you playing around,' he said. 'I am prepared to give and take a little, but I am not going to be cuckolded.'

'I won't play around on you,' she said, looking at

him with a cat-that-got-the-cream-and-the-canary smile. 'I'll be too busy counting my money.'

'If you don't behave yourself, there will be consequences,' Nic said. 'One false move and you will be out without a penny. It's written in the will. We both have to remain faithful, otherwise we automatically nullify the terms set down by my grandfather.'

'You will have to be *very* discreet then, won't you?' she asked with an arch look.

'You don't think I can do it, do you?'

She pulled her long black hair over one of her shoulders in a mermaid-like arrangement. 'Do what?' she said. 'Stay celibate? No, quite frankly, I don't. Who is your latest lover, by the way? Is it still the Brazilian heiress, or have you got someone else by now?'

His lips jammed together for a moment as if he was biting back a retort. 'A year without sex is a long time, Jade, for both of us. I can't see why we can't have our cake and eat it too.'

Jade rolled her eyes at his play on words. 'I

want the money, not you, Nic. I thought I had made that perfectly clear.'

'You say it with your mouth but not with your eyes,' he said. 'I give it a month at the most before you have them in sync. It's all part of the game, isn't it? It's what you do to every man: make them want you so badly they forget about promises and principles.'

'I can see you think you know me inside out,' she said. 'At least there won't be any nasty surprises once we are married.'

'I am afraid we will have to have a full-on wedding with all the regalia,' he said after a short tense pause. 'I hope that is not going to be a problem for you. It's just that my family will expect it and so will the public.'

'Fine,' Jade said. 'But I am not going to wear white or a veil.'

He tilted his head at her, a smile teasing the edges of his mouth upwards. 'You're not thinking of wearing black, are you?'

Jade held his look with defiance. 'I'm not

a virgin, Nic. I am not going to pretend to be something I am not.'

He frowned as if he found her statement somewhat bewildering. 'I don't recall saying that was a requirement of this arrangement. When it comes down to it, I am no angel myself. I probably should be ashamed to say this but I have lost count of the lovers I have had. You can probably still do a reasonably accurate tally.'

'Nope,' she lied, inspecting her nails. 'I've lost count too. Ages ago.'

The silence pulsed for a beat or two.

She looked up to find him watching her with a brooding expression. 'Is there anything else?' she asked. 'Any more tedious little rules I have to abide by?'

'No,' he said, snatching up his jacket and shrugging himself into it. 'That will be all for now. Just leave the press to me. I will handle the questions.'

Jade uncrossed her legs and got to her feet. 'Yes, Master,' she said and flicked the fine chain strap of her evening purse over her shoulder as she walked with swaying hips over to the door.

'Careful, Jade,' he warned. 'One step out of line and the deal's off. And don't think I wouldn't do it.'

Jade refused to let him see how unnerved she was by his threat. He might be calling her bluff but how could she know for sure? Of course she needed the money much more than he did. He had plenty of his own while she had nothing. But a year was going to change all that. She would finally be independent of her father. She would no longer need anyone's largesse to survive. She schooled her features into meekness. 'I will be a good girl, Nic, you just watch me.'

CHAPTER THREE

THEY had barely stepped outside the hotel on the Grand Canal when the paparazzi swarmed upon them. A journalist pushed a microphone towards Nic and asked, 'Signor Sabbatini, the news of your engagement and impending marriage to Ms Sommerville has taken everyone by surprise. You must have been conducting a very secret liaison. Do you have any comment to make about your romance?'

Nic smiled charmingly but Jade could tell he was grinding his teeth behind it. 'Ms Sommerville and I have been family friends for years. We finally decided to become more than friends. We are very much looking forward to our wedding next month. Now, if you'll allow us to celebrate our engagement in private, please move on.'

One of the older journalists pushed forward a

microphone in Jade's direction before Nic could do anything to block it. 'Ms Sommerville, you were involved some months ago with Richard McCormack, the husband of one of your best friends. Do you think the news of your engagement to Nic Sabbatini will finally repair your relationship with Julianne McCormack?'

Jade felt the subtle tightening of Nic's fingers around hers. 'I have no comment to make on any issue to do with my private life, apart from being very happy about my engagement to Nic. It's the best thing that's ever happened to me. I am so—'

'Excuse us.' Nic took command and led her through the crowd of tourists who had gathered.

'I thought I told you to leave the questions to me,' he said in an undertone as they weaved through the knot of people.

'Everyone will think it strange if I don't say something,' Jade argued. 'This is a momentous occasion, after all.'

He gave her a quelling look before heading for a restaurant on one of the canals.

They were led to a table in a lavishly appointed private room. Crystal chandeliers twinkled from the ceiling, plush velvet covered the chairs and hung from the windows in thick curtains in a rich shade of scarlet. There were Venetian masks on the wall, each one a work of art. The atmosphere was one of intimacy and privacy, and again Jade wondered how many women Nic had entertained here, wining and dining them before taking them back to his penthouse apartment to pleasure them. Strangely, she felt a jagged spike of jealousy poke at her and she shifted in her chair. Why would she be jealous? There would always be other women with Nic. It was the way he was made. He was not cut out for commitment and continuity in his love life. He was a playboy with a PhD in seductive charm. He could have anyone he wanted. He *had* had anyone he wanted.

The menus were placed in front of them and within minutes a bottle of champagne arrived in a silver ice bucket. Jade looked at it with wariness.

She had already had one more glass than usual. Being with Nic had the same effect as alcohol. It had made her head spin to see him dressed in nothing but his black underwear back there at the hotel. She had set out to be as brazen as she could—getting dressed in front of him to show him she was just as the press reported her—but it was completely different when he had done the same to her. She had tried not to look at his carved to perfection body. She had seen plenty of male bodies on the beach or at the gym, and some of them had been downright gorgeous. But something about Nic's always made her heart race and her senses tingle in a way they never did with anyone else. It made her feel deeply unsettled. She was the one who played the cat and mouse game with men, not the other way around. She didn't like the thought of Nic having that much power over her, in fact *any* power over her.

The attentive waiter filled both of their glasses before moving away to leave them in privacy.

Nic picked up his glass and raised it to hers. 'Let's drink to our first year of marriage.'

Jade gave him an ironic glance. 'Don't you mean the *only* year of our marriage? Don't the terms of the will state we have to be married by the first of next month and stay married for exactly a year?'

He drank from his glass before he answered. 'Yes, but what if we enjoy being married to each other? What if it turns out to be more convenient than we first thought? We could make it last as long as we like.'

Jade sat back in her seat as if he had pushed her backwards with one of his strong hands against her chest. 'You can't mean that!' she gasped.

He gave her one of his white-toothed smiles. 'Only teasing,' he said, his hazel eyes twinkling. 'Once the year is up next May, we can both take the money and run.'

Jade worked hard at squashing her sense of pique. She knew his motive for marrying her was only to get the money he felt entitled to; after all, she was doing it for the very same reason. She could hardly blame him for going ahead with his grandfather's stipulations. His two older brothers had had no such conditions placed upon them, but then Giorgio and Luca were both happily married with children. Giorgio and Maya had separated for a time, but had reconciled just before the old man's death. It had been Salvatore's desire to see all of his three grandsons settled before he died, but when he became ill so suddenly he had obviously decided to take matters into his own hands and make sure Nic bowed to pressure to settle down instead of playing the field for too much longer. Why Salvatore had chosen her as Nic's bride was a mystery. He could not have been unaware of the enmity between them. For the last decade they had snarled and sniped at each other when they had to be together at Sabbatini or Sommerville functions.

Jade knew a lot about the history of the Sabbatinis, having been a part of their circle for so many years. Her Australian-born father had befriended Salvatore when he was just starting out as an accountant and, with his Italian friend's help, his small accounting firm had become one of the most prestigious in Europe.

Like Nic and his brothers, Jade had grown up brushing shoulders with the rich and famous. Celebrities were not idols from afar; they were friends and acquaintances who regularly attended the same parties and social gatherings.

Jade's mother, Harriet, had been a London socialite herself until her untimely death from an overdose when Jade was five. Whether it had been suicide, a cry for help or an accident was something Jade and her brother Jonathan had never been told. There had always been speculation regarding Jade's parents' marriage. Throughout their childhood, it had been a case of don't-mention-your-mother-in-your-father's-presence by all the nannies and au pairs that had come and gone. Whether it would upset their father because of unresolved grief or anger was another mystery that had never been solved.

Jade looked at the menu and chewed her bottom lip in concentration. She hated eating out; it was something she usually avoided, but not for the reasons everyone assumed. It had been splashed all over the papers enough times—how she had been admitted to a special clinic when she was fifteen and then again at eighteen when she had skirted with death as her weight had dropped to a dangerously low level during the months following Jonathan's death. She was well and truly over all that now, but eating out still threw up the problem of how to choose when she had no idea what was written on the menu.

She felt Nic's gaze on her now, the weight of it like a stone. She looked up and closed the menu. 'What are you thinking of having?' she asked.

'The crab fettuccine to start with and maybe the veal Marsala for mains,' he said. 'What about you?'

Jade ran her tongue over her sand-dry lips. 'Why don't you choose for me?' she said, pushing the menu to one side. 'You seem to know the place pretty well. I'm not fussy.'

He cocked one of his eyebrows at her. 'No?'

'I've dealt with a lot of stuff over the years, Nic,' she said, giving him a hard look. 'I'm not going to embarrass you by dispensing with my meal in the bathroom as soon as your back is turned.'

A frown appeared between his brows. 'I wasn't suggesting any such thing,' he said. 'It was a tough time for you growing up, losing your mother so young and then your brother like that.'

Jade had perfected her back-off look over the years and yet, as she used it now, it was with shaky confidence that it would work. 'I'd rather not talk about it. They died. Life goes on.'

The waiter arrived to take their order, and when he left Nic shifted his mouth in a musing pose and continued to study her. She began to feel like a specimen under a powerful microscope. Nic always made her feel like that. He saw things that other people didn't see. His eyes were too all-seeing, too penetrating. It made her feel vulnerable and exposed—something she avoided strenuously at all times and in all places.

'Do you see much of your father?' Nic asked.

She toyed with the stem of her champagne flute, her eyes averted from his. 'Before this latest blow up, yes. He called in occasionally with his latest girlfriend,' she said tonelessly. 'The last one is only a year or two older than me. I think they might eventually marry. He wants a son—to replace Jonathan. He's been talking about it for years.'

Nic heard the pain behind the coolly delivered statement. 'You've never been close to him, have you?'

She shook her head, still not meeting his eyes. 'I think I remind him too much of my mother.'

'Do you remember her?' he asked.

Her jade-green eyes met his, instantly lighting up as if he had pressed a switch. 'She was so beautiful,' she said in a dreamy tone. She picked up her glass and twirled it gently, the bubbles rising in a series of vertical lines, each one delicately exploding on the surface. 'She was so glamorous and always smelt so divine—like honeysuckle and jasmine after a long hot day in the sun.'

She put the glass down, and ran her finger around the rim, around and around as she spoke.

'She was affectionate. She couldn't walk past Jon or me without encompassing one or both of us in a crushing hug. She used to read to me. I loved that. I could listen to her voice for hours…'

A little silence settled like dust motes in the space between them.

She gave a little sigh and picked up her glass again, twirling it before she took a tentative sip. She put it back down, her mouth pursing as if the taste of the very expensive champagne had not been to her taste. 'She loved us. She *really* loved us. I never doubted it. Not for a moment.'

Nic knew a little of the rumours surrounding Harriet Sommerville's death. There was some talk of an illicit affair that had gone wrong and Harriet had decided to end it all when the other man involved refused to leave his wife. Other rumours suggested Jade's father had not been the best husband and father he could have been at the time, but it was hard to know what was true and what had been fiction.

The press had a way of working it to their advantage: the bigger the scandal, the better the sale of the papers. Nic had experienced it himself, along with his brothers. But there was something about Jade that intrigued him. At regular intervals over the years she appeared at all the right functions, dressed to the nines, playing to the cameras, flirting with the paparazzi, but still he wondered if anyone really knew who the real Jade Sommerville was. Not the slim, beautiful and elegantly dressed and perfectly made-up young woman who sat before him now, twirling her champagne flute without drinking any more than a sip or two, who refused to speak of her dead brother, who spoke of her father with thinly disguised disgust.

Who was she?

Who was she *really?*

Was she the woman who had broken up the marriage of her best friend, as the papers had reported?

Or was she someone else entirely?

'Losing a parent is a big deal,' Nic said to fill the cavernous silence. 'I was knocked sideways by my father's accident. Seeing him like that...' he winced as he recalled it '…one minute so vitally alive, the next in a coma.' He raked his fingers through his hair. 'It was a relief when he died. No one wanted to say it but it was true. He would have hated being left with brain damage.'

She looked up at him with empathy in her eyes. 'You are a lot like him,' she said gently. 'I suppose lots of people have said that to you before. He hated being tied down.'

Nic smiled wryly as he picked up his glass. 'My parents' marriage was an arranged one. Not a lot of people know that. My mother loved him from the start but he was not so keen on being shackled to one woman. They muddled along as best they could until Chiara came along. My father loved having a daughter. He had three sons but his daughter was everything to him.'

He put his glass down with a clunk on the table, his eyes moving away from hers. 'Losing her was like the bottom of his world falling out from under him. He felt he was being punished by God for not loving his wife and sons enough. He went through a tumultuous time. As young as you were, I am sure you heard of it: numerous affairs with shallow gold-diggers until he finally realised the only woman he could love was the mother of his still living children who had loved him the whole time.'

'Everyone reacts to grief in their own way,' she said softly.

Nic picked up his glass but not with any intention of drinking from it, more for something to do with his hands. 'I am like my father in that I do not like to be told what to do,' he said. 'He always had issues with my grandfather over that. I guess that is why Salvatore's will was written the way it was.'

'But you are doing what he wanted now and that is all that matters,' she said in the same emotionless voice. 'In a year you will be free. You will have your inheritance and you can be with whoever you want.'

'So what about you?' Nic asked, raising his glass to his lips. 'What will you do once the year is up?'

She looked down at her hardly touched

champagne. 'I haven't thought that far ahead.' She looked back at him and gave him a forced-looking smile. 'I guess we will divorce amicably and get on with our lives.'

Nic wondered who she would want to spend her life with or if she wanted to settle down at all. If it hadn't been for his grandfather's machinations, at some stage she would have had to marry and to marry well. She had never worked a day in her life. She was a full-time socialite, born to it like others were born to poverty and neglect.

Until the withdrawal of her father's support, she certainly hadn't given Nic any indication that she was going to abide by the stipulations set down in the will. Nic had wanted to talk to her about it at length after the funeral, but when he had mentioned it during the service she had glared at him and then later slipped out before he could corner her. He certainly didn't see himself as qualifying for husband of the year or anything, but as long as she behaved herself he would put up with the twelve months of matrimony to secure his inheritance and thus keep his brothers' interests in the Sabbatini Corporation secure.

There were certain compensations in marrying Jade, of course. She was certainly a pleasure to look at. She had the most beautiful piercing green eyes, large and almond-shaped and darkly lashed, as thick as the silky, wavy hair that cascaded halfway down her back. With cheekbones you could ski off and a mouth that promised sensuality in every plump curve, she could have modelled if she'd put her mind to it, but for some reason had rejected an offer from a top agency when she was nineteen. Apparently she had been more than content to continue to live off her father's fortune, no doubt expecting it all to land in her lap on his demise some time in the future.

Yes, she was a gold-digger in her own way, Nic thought. She just did it a little more openly and shamelessly than most. It would be exciting having her in his bed. The more he thought of it, the more he longed to get down to it. She played it so cool but he could feel the heat of her passionate nature simmering underneath the surface. She was a born tease. She was deliberately ramping up his desire for her. She was a wildcat, a tigress that needed to be tamed and he would gladly be the one to do it and sooner rather than later, no matter what silly little hands-off-the-goods deals she insisted on making. He saw it for the ruse it was. She had wanted him since she was a hormone-charged sixteen-year-old and, because he had rejected her, she had played hard to get ever since.

'You do realise we will have to live together in Rome for most of the year, don't you?' he said after a pause. 'Apart from the times we travel.'

Her eyes flew to his. 'Travel? You expect me to travel with you?'

'That is what loving wives do, is it not?' he asked.

Her neatly groomed brows moved close together. 'But surely that's not necessary in our case. You're a busy man. You don't need a wife hanging off your arm in every city you travel to. Besides, I have things of my own to do.'

He hooked one brow upwards. 'Like what? Lime and vodka mornings and getting your hair and nails done?'

Her fingers tightened around her glass so hard Nic wondered if the fragile stem might crack. 'It's not that at all. I just like sleeping in my own bed.'

'Not according to what I read in the papers a few months ago,' he pointed out wryly. 'You were in and out of Richard McCormack's bed day in and day out while his wife's back was turned.'

She gave him a hateful glare. 'So you believe there is truth in everything written about you and your brothers in the papers, do you?'

He studied her for a moment. 'Not everything, no, but you didn't deny it. You could have slapped a defamation case on the paper if there was absolutely no truth in anything that was reported.'

'I have no interest in suing anyone,' she said. 'It's not worth the bother. They would just read it as defensiveness which, in my opinion, reeks of guilt. I've always felt it better to ignore it all and hope it eventually dies down.'

'It hopefully will now that we are about to be married,' he said. 'Have you a preference for a church wedding?'

She averted her gaze. 'No preference at all.'

'Then you won't mind if we have the ceremony and honeymoon in Bellagio?' he asked.

Her eyes came back to his. 'That's where your family has a villa, isn't it?'

'Yes.' He refilled their glasses before he added, 'It's also where my baby sister died all those years ago.'

Jade picked up her glass again. 'Well, then, it seems rather fitting to conduct a dead marriage there, doesn't it?'

His hazel eyes bored into hers for a tense moment. 'Your tongue is razor-sharp this evening,' he observed. 'You are the one who insists the marriage is to be in name only.'

'I don't love you, Nic, and you don't care a fig for me,' she said. 'We're only marrying each other to access a rather large fortune. That's about as dead as a marriage can be, is it not?'

'It doesn't have to be that way,' he said. 'We can work things to the advantage of both of us.'

She rolled her eyes at him. 'I can see how your mind works, Nic. You're already straining at the leash of imposed fidelity, aren't you? I told you: have your affairs if you must but keep them private. I don't want to be made a fool of in the press.'

'Same goes,' he said, leaning forward menacingly. 'I am warning you, Jade. If I hear one whisper of a scandal of you with another man, money or no money, our marriage will be terminated immediately, irrespective of what's written in the will. I am going to have it written into the prenuptial agreement.'

'Don't you mean our marriage will be annulled rather than terminated?' she asked with an arch look.

His eyes held hers like high-beam searchlights for so long Jade felt her skin break out in tiny goosebumps of apprehension. There was a steely purpose to his expression. He was not a man to be pushed around. Somehow he had turned the tables on her. She was not the one calling the tune here now, he was, and he was not going to allow her forget it. He had made it clear he desired her but she couldn't help feeling she was just going to be a convenient fill-in while he waited for his inheritance to be secure. Although she had tried her very best to disguise her response to him, it had clearly been to no avail. But then maybe he was like a lot of men even in these more enlightened times who still thought it their right to sleep with a woman who took their fancy: an expensive dinner, an even more expensive bottle of champagne and the transaction was settled.

Jade had determined she would not allow herself to be intimate with Nic. But somehow in the last couple of hours her resolve had been challenged in a way it had never been before. She saw the heat of desire in his eyes, the way his sexy mouth tilted in a lazy smile, as if he could already taste the victory of having her mouth plundered by his so very experienced one. She shifted uncomfortably on her chair, aware of her body in a way that made her feel distinctly uneasy about her ability to be immune to his sensual power. Her breasts felt full and tingly, her legs trembling and sensitive, as if they longed to be entwined with the length and strength of his in an erotic embrace.

He reached out and unpeeled her rigid fingers from around the stem of her glass. He brought those very same fingers up to his mouth, where suddenly they loosened and trembled, as if his breath contained a magic potion that unlocked every stiff joint, making them like putty in his hold. She sat transfixed, locked in a stasis that felt so strange to her and yet totally, inexplicably irresistible. She didn't want to break the spell. His eyes were holding hers in a lockdown that was unbreakable. She couldn't look away if she wanted to. Something was drawing her to him, like a silly little unsuspecting moth heading towards a bright hot light. She was going to get burned, but it was as if she didn't care. She drew in an uneven little breath as his lips brushed against the tips of her fingers, a barely touching movement that made her instantly ache for more.

'Why are you still fighting what has always been between us, Jade?' he asked in a low husky tone.

'I don't want to complicate things, Nic,' she said in a voice that sounded like someone else's, breathy, excited, anticipatory and expectant.

'You wanted me when you were sixteen,' he reminded her, nibbling on her fingertips again, a feather-touch of temptation—a lighted taper to her simmering need.

'I...I was young and you were—'

'Lusting after you but old enough to realise you were far too young to know what you were doing,' he said, smiling in a self-deprecating way. 'Jailbait Jade. That's what I nicknamed you. Did you know that? I daren't touch you for years after that. Not even a kiss on the cheek at any of the family gatherings. I didn't trust myself to take what had been on offer. I was seven years older than you. At twenty-three I had to be the adult, even though I wanted you like a raging fever in my blood.'

Jade pulled her hand away from his mouth,

tucking it safely away in her lap. 'I wish you would stop reminding me of how stupid I was back then,' she said, her eyes downcast.

'It's still there, isn't it, Jade?' he said in a smouldering tone. 'The hint of the forbidden, the lust, the longing, the need that won't go away. I see it in your eyes; I feel it in your body. I feel it like a pulse in my flesh when you look at me. We won't last the year without consummating this marriage and you damn well know it.'

She dared to look at him then, her heart giving a little pony kick in her chest. He meant it. He wanted her and he was going to do what he could to have her. She would have to be so strong, so very strong. Falling in love with Nic was the one thing she must not do. She had done it once before and look where that had taken her. It had set her life on a completely different course. She only had herself to blame, deep down she knew that. She had wilfully thrown away her innocence to get back at Nic and it had backfired on her terribly.

'My grandfather would not have tied you up in

this marriage unless he thought it was the best thing for you,' Nic said. 'He always made allowances for you, in spite of what was reported in the press. He defended you many times.'

Jade pushed the starter around her plate without getting any of it to her mouth. 'He was a good man,' she said softly, trying not to allow the mist of tears to break through. 'I have never quite understood how he and my father became such good friends. They were so very different.'

'Your father took the death of Jonathan very hard,' Nic said. 'Some people don't handle grief very well. I think my grandfather understood that, having lost his granddaughter and seeing his own son deal with it in his own way. There is no right way of doing it. We each have to find the right way to handle it—to learn to live with it.'

Jade looked up at him again. 'In my father's opinion, the wrong child died,' she said in a flat, emotionless tone that belied what she was feeling, what she had always felt.

Nic frowned, his dark brows so close together

they were almost joined above the bridge of his nose. 'Surely you don't think that? It was an accident. It could have happened to anyone. There was nothing you could have done to change that. There was nothing anyone could do. I told you before: you were lucky you weren't there with him.'

Jade gave a little shrug that said so little and yet so much. She had been the one who had caused Jonathan's death. He wouldn't have gone to such a challenging ski run if she had been with him because she wasn't as confident a skier. He had always watched out for her, staying with her even though he would probably have preferred to do his own thing. She had always maintained she had missed that flight because of her partying, but it had actually been because she had not properly memorised the itinerary her father had given her and had turned up at the wrong airline counter. By the time she had run across to the right one, it had been too late because the flight had already left. The shame of her inadequacy had kept her from asking the check-in staff to book her on another flight. It had all been too much so she had simply gone home and left a message for Jon to say she had changed her mind and was going to stay home and party instead. She was dumb and stupid—a dunce, as her father had so often told her. It was all her fault Jon had died that day and she had to live with it.

'Jade?' Nic reached for her hand but she moved it away from the glass she had been reaching for.

Drinking had been one of her coping mechanisms in the early days and it hadn't worked. It had hurt her rather than healed her. 'It's all right,' she said, giving Nic a rough version of a smile. 'Life goes on. Jon wouldn't have wanted me to waste my life bemoaning the past. He died the way he lived: on the edge, with loads of adrenalin, with laughter and courage and conviction.'

'So how do you live your life?' Nic asked.

With fear, apprehension, self-loathing and a truckload of regret, Jade thought, but didn't say. She pasted a plastic smile on her face and met Nic's dark, serious hazel eyes. 'I want to live the high life,' she said. 'I want money and lots of it. I want to never have to work, to not have to grind away at a job I loathe for the next forty-odd years and then retire to tend tomatoes and orchids or whatever it is that old people do these days.'

'Most of them spend time with their grandchildren,' he said.

Jade lifted her brows at him in a pert manner. 'Is that what you, the eternal playboy, plans to do?'

He frowned again, as if he had never given the idea much thought. 'Don't get me wrong,' he said. 'I adore my niece and two nephews. I can see the joy they bring to my brothers' and mother's lives. But I have never really envisaged a family life for myself. I travel all over the world at a moment's notice. My job in the Sabbatini Corporation requires it, especially now with Giorgio and Luca wanting to spend more time with their families. I am only home about one week in three.'

Jade felt a quake of unease pass through her. 'So you're expecting me to accompany you on *all* of those trips?'

He shifted his tongue inside his cheek, obviously giving it some thought. 'Not all, perhaps, but most. We are meant to be giving the impression of a solid and secure marriage, Jade. We can't do that if one of us is globetrotting on business and the other is lazing by the pool or heading off to the nearest health spa.'

She flashed him a vitriolic look. 'Is that what you think I do with my time?'

He picked up his glass and downed the contents before answering. 'You don't work, you don't volunteer, and you attend only the parties that suit your ends. I have no idea what you do with your time. Why don't you tell me?'

Jade thought of her canvases, back at her flat, in her makeshift studio in the small spare bedroom. How she had worked so hard to make up for her other failings. She hadn't sold anything and, like most artists, knew she might never make a decent living out of her creativity, but she secretly longed to. She longed to with a passion that was no doubt as strong as her father's drive to be the best accountant in the business. It was another one of her secrets, a passion she kept to herself in case it failed, thus proving to one and all that she was nothing but a shallow socialite with nothing to offer but a blueblood pedigree. Like her mother, she wasn't supposed to have a brain or a goal. She was meant to be on hand with the canapés and the champagne and the convivial conversation, working the room, aiming the shining beacon on her husband's stellar achievements.

But Jade had always wanted more. The trouble was, the more she wanted, the more likely it was to be taken away from her.

Like Nic…

She pulled away from her wayward thoughts, reminding herself sternly of Nic's motivations. He only wanted what he could get out of her by keeping her as his wife for the appointed time. Within a month they would be officially married. They would be on their way to having what they wanted: the inheritance. For Nic she was a bonus thrown in for free. He had a fantasy about her that stemmed from that silly little school-girl crush she had subjected him to. What full-blooded man wouldn't want to revisit that hotbed of almost but not quite ripe sensuality? But what Nic didn't know was that she was not really at heart that hardened hormone-driven harlot. What would it be like for him to see her as she really was instead of how the press portrayed her? Ha! As if he would have any respect for her if she revealed all.

'I like my life,' she said, not quite meeting his eyes. 'I know it's not for everybody but it suits me.'

'You are only…what, almost twenty-six? You are in the prime of your life. Have you no desire to do something with your intellect? Perhaps do some sort of course or degree?'

She gave him a bored look. 'I hated school so I can't see myself signing up for anything academic. I haven't got the discipline for it. Jon was the brains of the family.'

'I am sure you are underselling yourself,' he said. 'I know Jonathan was brilliant but you come from the same nest. You have the same blood running through your veins. It's just a matter of finding what you enjoy and are good at doing.'

'Don't worry about me,' she said with a dismissive wave of her hand. 'I will be quite happy being a social butterfly while you are off doing what you have to do.'

'Are you even interested in what it is I do?' he asked.

Jade felt a tiny stab of guilt she couldn't quite explain. 'You do something with the Sabbatini hotel chain,' she said, suddenly feeling hopelessly inadequate. 'Aren't you the financial controller or something?'

His eyes flickered upwards as if in disbelief or frustration or perhaps a bit of both. 'That is my brother Giorgio's role. I am the property developer. I scope out new real estate for development, some for hotels and others for our family investment portfolio. I am working on projects in several countries.'

Jade thought of all those hotel rooms, all those beds and bathrooms she would have to share with him in order to keep the truth of their convenient marriage a secret. One could possibly trust a long-serving household servant to keep that sort of confidence, but not the staff in a hotel, even a luxury Sabbatini one where the staff were rigorously hand-picked. 'Have you thought about the logistics of all of this?' she asked. 'We can hardly have separate rooms everywhere we go. People are bound to speculate and talk.'

He smiled at her in that seductive way of his that made her blood bubble with excitement in her veins. 'Do you really think you won't be begging me to bed you by the time we are married, or is this all just an act to whet my appetite?'

She tightened her mouth. 'It's no act, Nic. This is a hands-off deal.'

He cocked his handsome head at her. 'Why do I get the feeling you are saying that for your benefit not mine?'

Jade felt a blush steal over her cheeks. 'I am saying it because I know what you are like. You are used to women falling over themselves to occupy your bed.'

He leaned forward, his forearms resting across the table, his eyes dark and challenging as they held hers. 'How about we make a little deal, Jade?' he suggested. 'In public I will have to touch you as any husband would touch his wife, but in private I won't lay a finger on you unless you give me the go-ahead with those seductive green eyes of yours. Not one finger, OK?'

Jade eyed him suspiciously for a long moment, her heart beating like a drum that was being played by someone not quite sure of the correct rhythm. Could she trust him to keep his word? More to the point: could she trust herself? 'O...K,' she said at last, her breath coming out a little shakily.

'Good.' He sat back and picked up the bottle of champagne and topped up both of their glasses. 'It looks like we have a deal.'

CHAPTER FOUR

THE press had gone by the time they left the restaurant. Jade quietly blew out a breath of relief as Nic walked with her back to his hotel. She worked the press when she needed to but there were times when she wished she could disappear into anonymity. The news of their impending marriage would be splashed over every paper by morning. That was well and good, for it would make Nic less likely to pull out of the arrangement. He wouldn't want to draw any attention to the terms of his grandfather's will. He had his fair share of the notorious Sabbatini pride. For a playboy such as him to be dragged kicking and screaming to the altar would be the epitome of having one's pride bludgeoned.

Nic placed a protective arm around her waist as they weaved their way through the tourist crowd.

Feeling that band of muscle against her was creating enough heat to start a wildfire. She could feel the way her body responded to his closeness, the way her thighs trembled when he stood in the hotel lift beside her, not quite touching, but close enough for her to feel the hot, hard male heat of his long strong legs.

He took out his mobile and began to fiddle with the keypad. 'For some reason I don't have your mobile number in my phone,' he said, glancing sideways at her. 'I've only got your landline. What's your number?'

Jade pressed her lips together for a moment. 'Um…I don't have a mobile phone.'

His dark brows met over his eyes. 'What—did you lose it or something?'

She hesitated before answering. 'I…I had one once but then I lost it and I didn't get around to replacing it.'

He was still looking at her as if she had just landed out of time from a couple of centuries back. 'Are you *serious*?' he said. 'You really don't have a mobile?'

She shook her head as the doors of the lift opened.

'I will get you one tomorrow,' he said and pocketed his phone as he held the door back with the barrier of his arm.

Jade felt as if a butter churn had started to work on overdrive in her stomach. 'Please don't,' she said, biting her lip when he looked at her quizzically. 'I'm embarrassed to admit it but I'm really a bit of a technophobe. I only just worked out how to use the phone I had when I lost it. I don't want to have to go through all of that again.'

'Jade.' He gave her that look—the look that made her feel as if she were just about to walk in on the first day of kindergarten. 'The newer models are extremely simple to use. I will talk you through it and you'll be amazed at how easy it is. It's the same as using a computer. A little kid can do it. My niece Ella is already great at playing one of the games on my phone and she's not even three.'

She gave a vague nod of acquiescence and stepped out past him.

'What's your email address, then?' he asked once they were inside the penthouse.

Jade felt her stomach tilt in alarm. She racked her brain to think of an excuse for why she didn't have an email address. How could she possibly read an email when she couldn't even write her own name and address? 'Um…I can't tell you offhand—I've just had it changed. I was having some trouble with loads of…er…spam. The technician thought it best to change my network server. I haven't quite memorised the new address. It's a little more complicated than my last one.'

'Just shoot me an email when you get a chance and I'll add you to my contacts,' he said and handed her a business card with his contact details on it.

Jade looked down at the card. It was like Nic: distinctive and bold. The card was embossed and she ran her fingertip over it, feeling each letter through her skin, her brow furrowed in intense concentration.

'Are you learning my numbers off by heart?' he asked.

She tucked the card away in her purse, keeping her expression blank. 'I have no interest in learning anything but how to navigate myself through life to my advantage,' she said. 'Marrying you is, unfortunately, the only way of my achieving self-sufficiency.'

Nic's eyes studied her with increasing intensity and disdain. 'You are as shallow and self-serving as the press makes out, aren't you?' he said. 'You don't even bother disguising it. All you want is money and plenty of it.'

Jade gave him a fabricated smile, the sort that any hard-nosed gold-digger would use with ease. 'We are on the same mission then, aren't we, Italian boy? We both want a fortune to land into our hands and we are both prepared to sacrifice our souls to get it.'

His mouth tightened into a hard, flat line. 'Let's just hope it's worth it in the end,' he said.

'I am sure it will be,' she said, but inside she was already trembling with doubt. 'You will get your inheritance and I will finally get my independence. What more could we both want?'

His eyes seared a fire trail into hers. 'That remains to be seen, doesn't it?' he asked. He nodded towards the big bed. 'Which side do you want?'

Jade felt her eyes flicker in alarm but quickly controlled it before he could notice. 'Call housekeeping for a roll-out bed. I'll sleep on that.'

'You're joking, surely?' he said. 'We have just announced our engagement. What do you think the hotel staff will think if we insist on sleeping in separate beds?'

Jade put on her sassy face. 'They'll think we're saving ourselves for our wedding night.'

He gave an amused snort. 'You really are a chameleon, aren't you, *cara*? One minute you're the hot-blooded harlot and the next you turn into a shy virgin.'

She turned for the bathroom but he caught her by the back of her dress, pulling her into the rock-hard wall of his body, his hands coming to rest on the top of her shoulders, his chest against her shoulder blades, his pelvis pressing into her buttocks, stirring every nerve into a frenzy of awareness, making her breath stall like a faulty engine.

This was the closest she had been to him in years.

She could feel the hardened probe of his growing erection. She could feel the hammering of his heart against her right shoulder.

Oh, dear God, she could feel her resistance crumbling. The brick wall of determination she had set up to resist him was being dismantled second by second. She was not used to feeling this out of control. She was usually the one who had all the power over men. They didn't have it over her. Not one of them.

Except this one…

Jade wondered what would happen if she turned around and pushed her mouth up to meet his. To slip her tongue in between those mocking lips of his, to show him how hard she could drive him to the very edge of control.

She wanted to.

But she didn't dare.

'You know, you really should have thought this through a little more carefully, Jade,' he said in a smouldering voice, his mouth far too close to her neck.

She felt the fine hairs on her body stand to attention, her skin lifting in a shiver. She felt the warm dancing breeze of his breath as he leaned in closer; it feathered over her skin like a fine sable brush over a canvas.

'You rushed here to Venice without thinking about how this would end tonight, didn't you, *mio piccolo*?'

Jade bit down on her lip as she felt him move against her buttocks. He was practically parting them with his swollen length. It was the most tantalising feeling, deliciously erotic and sexy. Her body felt on fire. Flames licked along her flesh. Her belly was quivering with a whirlpool of need. Her inner core was throbbing like a heavy pulse that came from deep inside her body, a place she had not even been properly aware of before. Her breasts were prickling with sensation, her nipples tight and aching as they pushed against the fragile lace of her bra. 'You said you wouldn't touch me unless we were in public,' she said, sucking in her breath as his teeth nipped just below her earlobe.

'I said I wouldn't touch you if you didn't give me the come on,' he said. 'But you just can't help yourself, can you, *cara*?'

Jade turned and stepped away from him, sending him a defiant look. 'If you are going to break the rules from day one, then so can I. I have my contacts. I will tell them everything. I will even tell them about some of your brothers' stuff. That will go down a treat with your family, don't you think?'

He looked down at her, his jaw tight to the point of whiteness at the edges of his mouth. 'One false move, Jade, do you hear me? One false move and you'll be begging for a living off the streets, right where someone with your guttersnipe morals and behaviour belongs.'

Jade met him stare for stare, anger ballooning in her chest at his cruelly taunting words. 'You

think you can control me, don't you, Italian boy?'
she goaded him right on back.

His nostrils flared as he fought to control his
temper. 'You can't even control yourself,' he
said with a look of disgust. 'You're a spoilt brat
who should have grown up a long time ago. No
wonder your father cut you off without a penny.
You're nothing but a prima donna who doesn't
know how to behave like a woman of class and
breeding.'

Jade swung her hand up towards his face but
he caught it mid-swipe, holding it in a cruel grip
that made tears spring to her eyes. She suddenly
had the most unexpected urge to cry. She hadn't
cried in years, not since Jon's funeral. She wasn't
going to break down in front of Nic. She was not
going to let him see how much he had hurt her.
No one could hurt her. She always made sure of
that. *No one.* She blinked her eyes, gritted her
teeth and wrenched her arm out of his. 'I have to
use the bathroom,' she bit out and stalked from
the room.

When she came out after repairing the damage

to her make-up, Nic was standing with a brooding expression on his face. 'I'm sorry,' he said. 'I shouldn't have spoken to you like that.'

She gave a careless shrug. She had been called far worse in the press but somehow coming from Nic the words had been so much more devastating to hear. She hoped he hadn't heard her snivelling like a baby in the bathroom. She had turned on the taps to drown out the sound, but she saw the way his hazel eyes had softened in remorse. 'Do you want me to leave?' she asked. 'I can go and stay in another hotel. No one will probably even notice.'

'No, don't do that,' he said, rubbing the back of his neck. 'You have the bed. I'll sleep on one of the sofas. There are spare pillows and blankets in the wardrobe.'

She chewed at her lip as she watched him prepare the sofa. He was going to have a terrible night's sleep on that because, as luxurious as it was, he was just too tall for it.

He was right, of course. She hadn't thought much past getting him to agree to marry her. She hadn't thought of what would come next. Her impulsive nature had got her into trouble too many times to count. When would she ever learn?

'Would you like a nightcap or something?' Nic asked once the sofa was made up.

Jade shook her head. 'No, I'll just go to bed. I'm really tired. I feel like I've been travelling all day.'

'I'll leave you to prepare for bed in peace,' he said. 'I'm going to go downstairs to use the business centre.'

Jade could see his slim laptop on the antique desk over near the window, which could mean only one thing: he wanted to avoid her. She could hardly blame him. 'Well, goodnight, then,' she said.

His eyes met hers briefly. 'Goodnight, Jade.'

She sank to the bed once he had closed the door. Her body felt so tired from her crying jag in the bathroom. She would give anything to just curl up in amongst those soft, smooth sheets and forget the world for eight hours. She looked at her half-unpacked suitcase. She looked at it for a long moment, chewing at her lip as she planned her next course of action.

She sprang off the bed and quickly gathered her things, packing them haphazardly back in the case and snapping it shut.

Nic could have his bed. She would be miles away by the time he got back to his suite. She wasn't going to spend even one night more than necessary with him.

It was far too dangerous.

Nic came back to the suite after midnight. He had a headache and a neck ache and he was still feeling a brute for the way he had spoken to Jade. She had covered it well but he knew she had gone to the bathroom to compose herself. She had been on the verge of tears. Tears he had provoked.

He couldn't remember ever seeing her cry, or at least not since her brother's funeral and even then she had kept it in until the last moment, when Jonathan's coffin was lowered into the ground. She had been hysterical and had to be sedated once they got back to the Sommerville estate. Nic had tried to offer comfort but, if anything, his presence had seemed to upset her all the more. In the end he had left early and had stayed away from her for over a year. He wasn't proud of that. He often wondered if her decline back into an eating disorder could have been averted by a little more support from those best known to her.

The suite was in darkness and he reached for the nearest lamp switch, not wanting to disturb her with a bright light suddenly coming on. The muted glow of the lamp illuminated the huge bed but it was empty. He swung his gaze to the made-up sofa but it was empty too. He drew in a sharp hiss of a breath and strode through to the bathroom but there was nothing there except a faint trace of her perfume. He came back out to the suite and raked his fingers through his hair when he saw her suitcase had gone. He checked all over the suite but she hadn't even had the decency to leave him a note. He swore in three languages and paced the floor, frustrated beyond description.

The scheming little minx had tricked him

into agreeing to marry her. There was no way he could pull out of it now and she damn well knew it. The press were running with it. It had already been broadcast online and on the radio. He had already had a call from his brothers saying how pleased they were that he was doing what their grandfather had wanted. Her little staged you-hurt-my-feelings act had been convincing, so convincing he had fallen for it hook, line and sinker and outboard motor to boot. Damn the little witch!

Jade had been back at her flat twenty-four hours when Nic arrived. She winced when he put his finger on the buzzer, holding it down relentlessly, knowing she would have to answer before one of the neighbours complained about the noise. She opened the outer door for him and waited with a pounding heart for him to make his way to her flat.

His short hard knock on her door sounded like a firearm being discharged.

She opened the door with a breezy smile of greeting. 'Hi, Nic.'

He strode past her, his mouth set in a rigid line. 'Have you seen the papers?' he asked, thrusting a bundle at her.

'I don't read the papers,' Jade said, wondering if he would pick up on the irony in her tone.

'We are officially engaged,' he bit out.

She gave him a bright smile. 'Yes, I know. Isn't it exciting?'

He glowered at her darkly. 'And, since we are officially engaged,' he went on as if she hadn't spoken, 'you will at all times act like a fiancée should act. That means you will not leave my hotel or apartment or villa or wherever we might be staying without telling me where you are going. Do you hear me?'

Jade raised her chin. 'I left because I didn't want you to have a bad night's sleep. You wouldn't have slept a wink on that sofa.'

He narrowed his eyes at her. 'Don't go pretending you did anything charitable back there in Venice. You got what you wanted and left. You didn't even leave a note. What sort of disgraceful show of manners is that? I was worried sick about you.'

Jade tossed her head. 'I bet you weren't. I bet you were furious I slipped out without you knowing.'

'You're damn right I was,' he said. 'I had the press on my tail all the way back to London. I had to think of some sort of reasonable excuse for why you weren't still with me.'

'How terribly taxing for you,' she said with a roll of her eyes.

This time she actually heard him grinding his teeth. 'You really are the most uncontrollable brat I have ever met.'

'And you are the most undesirable fiancé a girl could ever want,' she threw back.

His hazel eyes flashed with green and brown flecks of hatred. 'I have organised a lawyer to come around this evening to go through the legal documents with you,' he said. 'I expect and demand your full cooperation in reading and signing them.'

Jade controlled her instinctive panic with an effort. 'I will do what is necessary to secure my inheritance but I will do nothing extra.'

'You will do as you are damn well told,' he said heatedly. 'I have decided to bring the wedding forward. I don't trust you to be out of my sight for the rest of this month. You will move to my villa in Rome as soon as it can be arranged. We will be married early next week. I have already informed my family of the change of plan.'

This time it was impossible for Jade to hide her panic. 'I…I don't want to do that…I have things to do here in London. I don't want to leave before I'm ready.'

'We do have hairdressers and nail technicians in Italy, you know,' he said with a sarcastic bite. 'We even have fashion designers.'

She sent him a fulminating glare. 'You can't have everything your own way, Nic. I know you have for most of your life, but I am not going to be pushed around by you.'

'I am sending a removal company for your things in the morning,' he said. 'The lawyer will be here in less than an hour. I have also organised a wedding planner to meet with you this evening. She will see to all details to do with the ceremony. We will travel together to Rome late tomorrow afternoon. I will send my driver to collect you. If you do not cooperate I will call the press and tell them the wedding is off.'

'You won't do that,' Jade said with not as much confidence as it sounded.

He held her gaze with steely intensity. 'Don't bet on it, Jade,' he said. 'I will do what I damn well please and you will obey without question.'

Jade picked up a cushion from the sofa and threw it at him. It missed by a mile and bounced off the wall without even making a sound as it fell impotently to the floor. 'I hate you,' she said. 'I really, *really* hate you.'

He smiled coolly as he opened the door. 'I hate you too; you have no idea how much.'

She winced as he closed the door on his exit. And for the second time in twenty-four hours she felt tears prickle and burn at her eyes.

CHAPTER FIVE

LESS than an hour later a lawyer arrived with papers in hand, just as Nic had informed her. Jade went through all the motions: politely offering coffee or tea, providing a seat at the dining table so the papers could be spread out easily, all the while hoping her façade of understanding everything would not be shown up for what it was: total ignorance.

'And if you will just sign here and here,' the lawyer said, pointing out the sections that were highlighted.

Jade scribbled her signature while inside cringing at how unsophisticated and childish it looked next to Nic's where he had signed earlier. She studied the bold strokes of his name; the confidence and assurance she always associated with him were there in every twist and turn of his pen.

Not long after the lawyer left a woman arrived, announcing herself as the wedding planner. Jade allowed herself to be swept up in the momentum of confirming all the appointments: the fitting of a dress at a designer studio once she got to Rome, a visit to the jewellers' where she would be fitted with an astonishingly expensive engagement and wedding ring ensemble that had already been chosen on her behalf, as well as a visit to a high street florist where the flowers for the church and the wedding bouquet would be chosen, ready to be flown to the church in Bellagio by private jet.

It was all done with the efficiency of clockwork but inside Jade was secretly worrying about the year ahead. She could look and dress the part of the happy bride but she was not the bride of Nic's choice.

They were both marrying under sufferance; it was a chore—it was a time line they both had to endure to get what they wanted.

Jade tried not to think of the romantic fantasies she had conjured up in the past. That was a long time ago and this was here and now. This was a cold, hard business deal, a transaction with financial rewards to be gained. It was not about love or mutual goals. It was about Nic Sabbatini inheriting what was rightfully his. She was the pathway for him to do that and he was hers. She was nothing to him but a means to an end and she would be a silly fool to think otherwise.

A courier arrived early the next morning and delivered a high-tech mobile phone to her apartment. He assured her it was already charged and ready to use. Jade signed for it and, after a long period of hesitation, she unpacked it from its packaging, not for the first time feeling all alone in the world, with no one to understand how desperately vulnerable she felt. She put it away in her handbag and got on with the rest of her packing in preparation for the move to Rome. The removal men arrived and took everything out of her flat. She hovered about as her paintings were being loaded, worried they would be damaged, but the men seemed to know what they were doing and covered everything in bubble wrap.

Nic called just before lunch to say he had to fly out of London for the rest of the week to sort out a property deal in Rio de Janeiro and she would have to go to Rome without him. 'I'm sorry about the short notice,' he said. 'But no doubt you'll have plenty to do preparing for the wedding.'

'I'm surprised you aren't insisting I accompany you,' Jade said somewhat waspishly, 'or is it because you have some unfinished business to do in the bedroom rather than the boardroom?'

'I thought you said you didn't read the gossip in the papers?' he said.

Jade ground her teeth, imagining him with the long-legged, exotic Brazilian model, having a last fling before their marriage. The trouble was, it would very probably not be his last. A man like Nic would not stay true to fake marriage vows; he would have trouble staying true to real ones.

'And I also thought you said I could do what I liked as long as I was discreet about it,' Nic added when she didn't respond.

Jade unlocked her tight jaw. 'Do what you like. I can't stop you. According to the lawyer you sent around, you've got your back well and truly covered.'

'Ah, so the prenuptial is a sticking point, is it?' Nic said.

'Do you really think I want half of everything you own?' Jade said. 'I just want what Salvatore wanted me to have.'

'Divorces can get pretty ugly, Jade,' he said. 'I am not prepared to risk all that my grandfather and father and two older brothers worked so hard for when we part company in a year's time. Don't take it personally. It's just sound business sense to protect one's assets.'

Jade knew what he said was true, and to some degree it was her own fault for encouraging his opinion of her as an empty-headed, gold-digging socialite.

'Did you get the mobile?' he asked after a tense pause. 'I tried calling you on it earlier but the message service said it was switched off. I made sure it was charged before it was delivered. Have you turned it off or something?'

Jade swallowed and looked in the direction of her handbag. 'Um…I haven't had time to answer it with all the packing I've been doing.'

'I have people organised to do that for you,' he said. 'Why are you doing it yourself?'

'I don't like strangers touching my things,' she said, turning her back on the accusing presence of her handbag.

There was another little silence.

'I probably won't see you until the day of the wedding,' he said. 'My business is taking longer than I expected. I have organised a private jet to take you to Rome. My driver will pick you up and take you to the airport. You will be driven to my villa and my housekeeper, Guilia, will help you settle in. The wedding planner will see to everything and will be in contact with you over the last-minute things. Your flat will be packed up and the keys handed back to your father. He has someone who wants to rent it as of next week.'

'Is he coming to the wedding?' Jade asked.

'Yes, he said he was looking forward to giving you away.'

Yes, well, it wouldn't be the first time, Jade thought bitterly.

Jade arrived, just as Nic had arranged, at his villa in Rome. It had been a relief to have someone see to all the travelling arrangements for once. She normally had to engage the services of a travel agent, which was always stressful as she had to memorise everything as the documents they handed to her in a file were useless. She envied everyone who could book things online. They didn't have to commit everything to memory and then worry incessantly in case they forgot a date or a time or an address. Visiting new places was an absolute nightmare for her. She had got lost so many times and felt so foolish when asking for directions, only to find she was just a street or a block away.

Rome was a place she was familiar with, so was Milan, but Bellagio was going to be a challenge; she hoped if she stayed close to the Sabbatini villa she wouldn't go far wrong. However, if Nic was really serious about taking her with him on all his trips abroad she would have to think of some way of coping. She couldn't wander around like a normal tourist, reading maps and street names. She would have to stay in the hotel and fill in the time rather than risk exposing her defect. She would rather die than have Nic know she was severely dyslexic. No one knew. It was her shameful little secret.

The housekeeper at Nic's villa was austere and unwelcoming right from the moment Jade stepped through the imposing front door. Guilia Rossetti gave Jade an up and down look that would have stripped a century of wallpaper from a wall. 'So this is Nicolò's future bride,' she said, making a guttural sound of disgust in her throat. 'He could have done much better. I read all about you. You're not worthy of the Sabbatini name. You will bring nothing but harm and shame to him and to the family, I am sure of it.'

Jade straightened her spine and stared down the dark-eyed Italian. 'If you want to keep working for my future husband, then I would advise you to keep your opinions to yourself.'

Jade pointed to the bags the driver had placed at the foot of the stairs. 'You can unpack for me and then I would like a gin and tonic brought up to my room, ready and waiting for me after my shower,' she said in a haughty tone.

The housekeeper's eyes were like black diamonds, beady and full of loathing. *'Sì, signorina,'* she said through gritted teeth and bent to snatch up the bags.

Jade tossed her hair over her shoulder and wandered through the villa. It was a glorious place, beautifully decorated with gold and marble, signalling the wealth Nic and his brothers had grown up with and most probably taken for granted, just as she had done until her supply of money had been stopped. She pushed the irritating thought aside and looked at the artwork on the walls, some of which she recognised from some of her favourite masters.

The villa was three storeys high and overlooked wonderful gardens, complete with a lap pool and jacuzzi and a tennis court. Jade walked out through a set of doors into the bright April sunshine. The water of the pool sparkled and a light breeze crinkled the surface. The lawn was a verdant expanse of green, lush and with that delicious fresh fragrance of having just been mown. A white wisteria was hanging in a scented arras from a stone wall, the hum of bees as they collected the sweet pollen filling the air. Roses were everywhere and in every shade imaginable: pinks and whites and whites blushed with pink, deep blood-red ones, mauve and yellow and apricot. The fragrance collectively was heady and intoxicating and she breathed deeply to take it in.

She walked a little farther and sat on a stone bench overlooking a fountain that had a marble Cupid figure pouring water from a pitcher which then overflowed to the base of the fountain. It was a peaceful, tranquil sound: the gentle splashing of water over centuries-old marble. The urge to paint the scene was overwhelming but she had to restrain herself as her things were still in boxes waiting to be unpacked.

When she went back inside the housekeeper was coming down the stairs. She gave Jade a caustic look. 'I have put your things in the yellow room,' she said. 'After the honeymoon I will move them into Signor Sabbatini's suite, but not before.'

Jade suddenly decided she would sleep in Nic's bed just to annoy the housekeeper. It wouldn't matter because Nic had already told her he wouldn't be back in Rome before the wedding and would meet her at the church in Bellagio. 'I am afraid you will have to do so for I am intending to sleep in my fiancé's bed,' she said with a don't-dare-to-disobey-me air.

The housekeeper muttered something in Italian before she stalked off, her footsteps clacking with anger across the marble floor.

Jade let out a breath and walked up the grand staircase, her footsteps muffled as they trod on the priceless stair runner held in place by solid brass bars at the back of each step.

She found Nic's room without any trouble. It was just as she had imagined it would be. It was huge, as was the bed, and it was decorated in brown and cream with a touch of black in the lamps and bedside tables, giving it an unmistakably masculine feel. The en suite bathroom was as big as her London flat's bedroom and it followed the same gold and marble theme of the rest of the villa.

The shower was refreshing but she couldn't help thinking of Nic's naked body standing right where she was standing. Her mind pictured him with the water cascading over him, over his chest and ridged abdomen, down his hair-roughened flanks and over his taut buttocks and the proud male heart of him. Her breath caught in her throat and she quickly turned off the water and reached for one of the big fluffy towels that was as big as a sheet.

When Jade came back into Nic's bedroom it was obvious the housekeeper had failed to bring her things through. She drew in an angry breath and stalked out to the landing. 'Guilia?' Her voice echoed through the villa. 'Will you come up here immediately and do as I asked you to do?'

There was no response.

Jade stormed to the yellow room and, dropping her wet towel on the floor, rummaged through the wardrobe for something to wear. She didn't bother drying her hair but left it loose to dry naturally. She didn't bother with make-up either. She never did if she wasn't expecting anyone to be around or she wasn't going out.

There was no sign of the housekeeper downstairs, although Jade did see a note propped up against the kettle. She looked at it, wondering what the housekeeper had written. The handwriting looked as if it had been done quickly and crossly, but if it was in Italian or English, she couldn't quite tell. She scrunched it into a ball and left it on the bench.

She filled in the rest of the evening by sorting some of her paints and sketchbook into a smaller bag to take with her to Bellagio. She had seen enough travel shows to know how picturesque the Italian lakes district was. It was the one part of her honeymoon—such as it was—she was looking forward to.

After a light supper of chicken and salad she

had found in the fridge, she made her way back upstairs to bed. The villa was scarily empty. There was no sound apart from the ticking of an ormolu clock on a French lacquered table on the second landing.

She slipped out of her jeans and loose-fitting top, her bra and knickers adding to the pile on the floor. The sheets were smooth and cool and fresh and, within seconds of putting her head down on the feather pillows, she felt her eyelids going down as if weighted by anvils...

Jade stretched out a leg and froze. Her eyes flew open and she sat bolt upright. 'What the hell are you doing here?' she asked as Nic opened one sleepy eye from right beside her.

He propped himself up on one elbow. 'Where else would I be?' he asked. 'This is my bed.'

'I...I know but you're not supposed to be here now!' she said, pulling her legs out of the reach of his long, strong hairy ones.

He sat up in the bed, the sheet that had been covering him slipping to just below his navel.

Jade saw the dark masculine hair that arrowed down beneath the sheet and her stomach did a jerky little somersault. He was as naked as she was. She could practically see the outline of his maleness.

'I came back by private jet after I got a call from my housekeeper,' he said. 'She refuses to work for me while you are in residence. What on earth did you say to her?'

Jade pushed her lips out in a pout. 'She was awful to me from the moment I stepped in the door. She refused to do what I asked and she called me horrible names.'

Nic pushed back the sheet and rose from the bed. Jade swallowed as she saw the masculine perfection of his body. He was so toned and taut, so powerfully male in every plane and contour.

He slipped on a lightweight bathrobe and tied the ends around his waist as he looked down at her in the bed. 'This has to stop, Jade. You can't act like this. Don't you understand? You have to take responsibility for your actions.'

'*My* actions?' she said indignantly. 'What about

hers? She's your employee so she should have more respect. It shouldn't matter who you marry. She should accept your future bride without question or snide and insulting comments.'

'I am afraid there are times in life when you have to earn respect,' Nic said. 'It doesn't come automatically just because of whom you are married to or how much you earn or where you were born.'

She gave him a mutinous scowl. 'I am not going to kowtow to the cleaning staff just so they'll be nice to me. I will do what I want.'

Nic grasped the end of the sheet and ripped it from the bed. He smiled at her shocked expression. She looked like an outraged virgin about to be ravaged by a devilish suitor. 'Do I have to teach you some manners myself, my naughty little wife-to-be?' he asked as he tugged her down by one ankle until she was lying between his open thighs as he stood at the end of the bed.

Her slim throat rose and fell and her breasts, which she had so brazenly flashed at him only days ago, she was now struggling to cover with her hands. Her cheeks were stained a delicate shade of pink and her eyes were wide and uncertain, their long dark lashes giving her a Bambi look that was totally captivating. 'Wh…what do you think you're doing?' she asked in a high-pitched strained sort of voice.

'I thought I might try the goods before I buy since they are right here in my bed for my pleasure,' he said, stroking his hand up the smooth length of her leg from ankle to calf. 'That was your intention, wasn't it? To get my attention? Well, you got it, baby. I am here and I am all yours.'

She tried to kick out at him but his fingers locked around her ankle. She kicked out with her other leg but he caught that slim ankle too and held it firm.

'Let me go, you arrogant bastard!' she said, struggling like a wildcat.

'Manners, Jade,' Nic said silkily. 'You will learn to speak to me with respect.'

Her face was a picture of rage, all flashing green cat's eyes and white teeth bared in a snarl.

'I'll never forgive you for this,' she said. 'If you lay even one finger on me I will scratch your damn eyes out.'

'I bet you say that to all your lovers,' he said with a mocking smile.

She fought him with a strength he didn't realise someone of her delicate frame could possess. She bucked and arched and jerked until he had to let go in case she hurt herself. She crawled away from him like a scuttling crab, scooping up the sheet he had tossed from the bed and wrapping it around herself like a shroud before she faced him with a blistering glare. 'If you think you can just do what you like when you like, you are sadly mistaken,' she said.

'Ditto, *cara*,' he said. 'It's time you learned how to behave, and if I have to teach you myself I will do it.'

Jade poked her tongue out at him.

He laughed. 'You are going to be absolute dynamite in bed. No wonder you have men following you with their tongues hanging out. I can't wait to see what fireworks we set off together.'

She gave him a cutting look. 'If you want to sleep with me you can damn well pay for it.'

'I have paid for it, Jade,' he said as he opened the door to leave. He gave her one last up and down stripping look and added, 'I paid for you with my freedom and I expect to collect on it as soon as we are officially married.'

Jade winced as the door closed on his exit. Surely he didn't mean it? He wouldn't insist on sleeping with her if she didn't want to. She bit her lip. The trouble was, she did want to.

She wanted to very much.

When Jade came downstairs the next morning Nic was swimming in the lap pool. She watched him from the windows of the breakfast room, his bronzed body carving the water like an Olympic athlete. He made her floundering efforts to stay afloat seem rather pathetic in comparison. It was another one of her failings. She had never learned to swim with any proficiency.

She turned away with a sigh and went to the

kitchen. Her supper things were still on the bench where she had left them, so too was a glass Nic had obviously used to have some orange juice before his morning swim. She gave a little shrug of indifference and turned away.

Nic came in through from the doors that led to the terrace. He was naked from the waist up, a towel hanging from his lean hips. 'Is breakfast ready yet?' he asked, pushing back his wet hair with one of his hands.

Jade frowned. 'Pardon me?'

He nodded towards the breakfast room. 'Coffee and fruit to start with and then some fresh rolls,' he said. 'I'll expect you to have it ready by the time I come back from my shower.'

She opened her eyes wide. 'Are you expecting *me* to wait on you?'

'Well, it was you who caused the housekeeper to leave in a huff,' he reminded her. 'It's only fair you take over her role until I can find someone to replace her.'

Jade bristled in outrage. 'I will do no such thing. Get your own stupid breakfast.'

He eyeballed her until she felt the base of her spine start to tingle. 'Breakfast, Jade, and step on it. I have an important meeting at my office this morning.'

She pressed her lips together, glaring at him, daring him to make her do his bidding. The air crackled with electricity as their strong wills collided. She felt the power of it, the tension escalating along with her heart rate. She was not going to be a slave to him. He was not going to order her about like some servant in his employ.

She smiled to herself as she planned her next move. She would show him just how little he could control her.

Nic came over to where she was standing. He stopped right in front of her, holding her defiant gaze with the steely determination of his. 'Do I have to repeat myself?' he asked.

Jade put on a meekly obedient face. 'It'll be ready in five minutes,' she said.

'Good girl,' he said and flicked her cheek with a gentle finger before he left the room.

* * *

Jade brewed some coffee and then sliced up some fruit and set it on a plate. She found the fresh rolls in a paper bag on the bench. She assumed someone from the bakery had delivered them earlier that morning. She carried a tray with everything on it into the breakfast room and set it out on the table that overlooked the sunny terrace.

Nic came in a few minutes later, straightening his tie. 'Nice job,' he said. 'I knew you could do it if you put your mind to it.'

'How do you have your coffee?' Jade asked, working hard at keeping her expression suitably subservient.

'White with two sugars,' he said as he sat down.

Jade put a cup down next to him and poured the coffee into it. Then she carefully spooned two teaspoons of sugar into it. She picked up the milk jug and said, 'Say when,' and then she poured the entire contents into his lap.

He leapt up from the table, his expression thunderous as he wiped at the dripping milk with a hastily grabbed napkin. 'You little bitch,' he growled at her.

Jade gave him a guileless look. 'You didn't say when.'

He tossed the sodden napkin aside and reached for her. Jade hadn't expected him to move quite so fast. Suddenly she was being held by the upper arms, his eyes blazing as they held hers.

Time stood still for the space of three rapid heartbeats.

And then with a muttered curse he swooped down and slammed his mouth down against hers.

Jade had lost count of the number of times she had been kissed. She had enjoyed some and hated others. But this was nothing like anything she had experienced before. Nic's mouth was like a flame against the soft flesh of her lips. It stoked a wildfire inside her, a raging fire that leapt and danced all over her skin. His kiss was bruising but she didn't care. She loved the taste of him, so fresh and male and commanding.

He cupped her head with his hands and

deepened the kiss with an erotic thrust of his tongue. Her belly flipped as it curled around hers, flicking, stroking, teasing, conquering.

The kiss went on and on.

She tasted blood but wasn't sure if it was hers or his. She had nipped at him just as frantically as he had nipped at her. Their teeth had even clashed at one point in the desire to gain supremacy. It was the most breathlessly exciting sensual assault on her senses. She felt as if she had been waiting her entire life for this moment. It was bliss to have his mouth hard and insistent on hers, the heated trajectory of his arousal burning like a brand against her.

But just as suddenly as it had started it was over.

Nic stepped away from her, wiping the back of his hand across his mouth, his breathing as ragged as hers. 'You had better make yourself scarce, young lady,' he said. 'I am so angry with you right now I don't trust myself to be around you.'

Jade ran her tongue over her swollen mouth,

wincing as she felt the little split in her lip. She saw him narrow his eyes as he looked at her mouth, a flicker of remorse passing over his expression.

'Damn it, Jade,' he said, raking his hair with one of his hands. He stepped close again and tipped up her face, a gentle fingertip tracing the tiny wound on her lip. 'Does it hurt?' he asked in a gruff tone.

'No,' she said in a whisper.

He slid his hand to the nape of her neck, holding her gaze for an endless moment. 'I'm sorry.'

'I'm sorry too.'

Nic dropped his hand from her neck and stepped back. 'I'm afraid I haven't got time to help you clear up here,' he said. 'I'm already running late and I have to change.'

'What time will you be home?'

'I'll call you and let you know. I might have to fly back to Rio. If so, I will meet you at Bellagio as previously planned.'

'Nic?'

He turned at the door. 'Yes?'

Jade twisted her hands together. 'I'm sorry about your housekeeper leaving.'

He gave her a brief crooked smile. 'Forget about it. I was thinking of firing her anyway. I think she's been filching the spirits.'

'Oh.'

'Why don't you check out the job seekers ads in the paper?' he said. 'That way you can interview all the candidates and decide who you'll get along with.'

Jade felt her chest tighten with panic. 'Oh, no, I can't do that.'

He gave her a frowning look. 'Of course you can, Jade. You just have to call them up and arrange a time to meet them.'

'But I can't read Italian.'

'You can do it online in English,' he said. 'There's a computer in my study. There are listings of all the employment agencies.'

'Can it wait until we get back from Bellagio?' she asked.

He looked at her for a long moment. 'Of course it can wait.' He walked over to the door, but then he paused with his hand on the doorknob as if a thought had suddenly occurred to him. He slowly turned and looked at her again. 'You do know how to use a computer, don't you?'

'Of course I do,' Jade said with a heavy dose of indignation. 'What do you think I am—completely brainless?'

'No, on the contrary, Jade, I think you are one of the cleverest people I have ever met. Not many people catch me off guard but you've done it not once, not twice, but three times. I wonder how many more surprises are in store for me during the next year.'

'You'll just have to wait and see, won't you?' she said with a pert look.

'I am looking forward to it,' he said and left the room.

CHAPTER SIX

As IT turned out, Nic did have to fly back to Rio, or so he had said when he'd phoned on the landline later that day. Jade wondered if he was putting some space between them after The Kiss. She couldn't help thinking of it in capital letters. Her lips had tingled for hours afterwards. Her tongue kept returning to the tiny nick in her flesh, exploring it in detail. It was a constant reminder of the spontaneous combustion that had occurred between them. Nic had awakened a longing in her that would not go away. It ached and throbbed deep and low in her body, a persistent ache of emptiness she had never felt before.

She spent a couple of quiet days painting in the villa gardens before the preparations for the wedding began in full force. The flight and travelling arrangements turned out to be far easier than she had expected and the wedding planner had taken care of all the details, so all Jade had to do was turn up for her hair and make-up appointment, and finally slip into her dress and shoes.

When she finally arrived at the church in the picturesque lakeside town of Bellagio she felt as if she was acting her way through a movie role directed by Nic. Her father walked her into the church, beaming at all the guests as if he was the proudest of men. Jade went along with the façade of family togetherness but, as she walked past the front pew where her brother most likely would have been if he had still been alive, she felt a pain that was indescribable.

She looked up and saw Nic standing at the front with the priest. His hazel eyes ran over her, his lips stretched into a proud smile, she assumed for the congregation's sake. Her heart gave a little skip as his eyes darkened the closer she got. She saw his gaze go to the now healed spot on her lip. His eyes came back to hers, a silent message there that touched her so much she had to look away. She faced the front and listened as the priest began to speak.

Jade was conscious that this was the very church in which Nic's baby sister had been christened and then just three months later farewelled from this world. The wedding planner had let slip that this was the first time Nic's mother had come back to the villa since Chiara's death all those years ago. Jade wasn't sure why Nic had insisted on being married here, other than the villa was very private and the perfect place to have a honeymoon. Not that they were having a honeymoon, of course, Jade thought. It was all for the press, the pretence, the society wedding with all the trimmings. It was what everyone expected someone of Nic's breeding, and hers when it came to that, to do.

Finally the priest announced it was now time for Nic to kiss his bride and Jade felt a ripple of excitement race through her. She swallowed as he slipped a hand to the curve of her cheek, his touch and gaze as tender as any genuine groom's could be. She watched in breathless anticipation as his head lowered inch by inch until finally she felt the whisper-soft press of his lips on hers.

Again Jade was totally sideswiped at how her mouth responded to his. It was as if he had transferred some potent electrical current directly from his mouth to hers. Her lips moved beneath the gentle press of his, softly and shyly at first but then more hungrily as he deepened the kiss with a slow, smooth thrust of his tongue that took her completely by surprise. While it was nothing like the primal savagery of his previous kiss, for some reason the tenderness of this one was even more powerful and mind-blowing. She felt a shockwave of heat envelop her, and her tongue moved against his, tasting him, tasting the essential maleness of his mouth. He tasted minty, fresh and yet hot and erotic and brooding with barely leashed sensuality.

He pulled away first, smiling down at her, saying in an undertone, 'Save it for later, *cara*, for when we are naked and alone.'

Jade felt her colour rise but could do nothing but smile back as she knew the congregation was watching every move she made. She had already heard the collective *'ahh'* in response to their kiss. She silently fumed at Nic's arrogance. Did he really think she would sleep with him just because they were now married? He had probably slept with his mistress only the day before. Her anger went up a notch. No wonder he had flown straight back to Rio. He had no doubt taken advantage of his last couple of days of freedom; the freedom he claimed was the price he had paid for her.

Jade knew he would be an unforgettable lover for all the right reasons. But allowing such intimacy between them would be a disaster for her in the long run. She was increasingly worried about her feelings for him; feelings that used to be hate were morphing into something else entirely—something that was far more dangerous. She had to keep reminding herself this was a temporary marriage and any relationship between them was going to be over as soon as Nic got what he wanted: his inheritance.

The reception was held back at the villa, where

a huge marquee had been set up in the gardens. Champagne flowed freely and Jade continued to play the role of blissfully happy bride—a role she found she could pull off with surprising ease, which was another worry to her—chatting with Nic's brothers and their wives and the other guests until her face ached from smiling so much.

At one point she looked across at Nic, who was cradling his baby nephew Matteo, Giorgio and Maya's son, in his arms. He was smiling at the gorgeous dark-haired baby, speaking in Italian while the baby cooed back in the universal language of young babies. Little Ella, Luca and Bronte's oldest child, was leaning against Nic's thigh, eagerly awaiting her turn for his attention. He turned and smiled at her adoringly, the words he spoke in his mother tongue obviously pleasing the little toddler, who grinned widely before saying something back in the same language with her own twist on the accent. Jade watched as he scooped Ella up in his arms, holding her high above his head, the toddler's squeals of delight filling the air.

'He'll make a fabulous father when the time comes,' Bronte said as she came over to where Jade was standing. 'He's such a natural with kids.'

Jade felt a blush flow like a tide into her cheeks. She swept her gaze around to check for hovering members of the press before she spoke in an undertone. 'You know this is not a marriage that is going to last. We're both in it for what we can get.'

Bronte's slate-blue eyes held hers. 'I know you care for him, even if you don't like admitting it,' she said softly.

Jade bit her lip and averted her gaze, staring at the untouched champagne in her glass. 'You're mistaken, Bronte. I hate him as much as he hates me.'

'I don't believe that,' Bronte said. 'I used to think I hated Luca but it was love all along. You and Nic are made for each other. Anyone can see it. You're both so stubborn, neither of you wants to be the first one to break.'

'I can't see Nic admitting to feeling anything

for anyone,' Jade said with a despondent sigh. 'He's never been one to talk of his feelings. He jumps from one woman's bed to another. I think the longest relationship he's ever had was less than a month.'

'Luca told me you used to have a crush on Nic,' Bronte said. 'Was he your first love?'

Jade turned and looked at Luca's lovely wife. No wonder he had tracked her down after he had finally sorted out his life. How he had torn himself away from her in the first place was something Jade still didn't quite understand. But they were so happy now and that was all that mattered. She envied them. She envied Giorgio and Maya too who, only moments before, had been looking at each other over by the fountain as if no one else was around. How she longed for that sort of love in her life. 'It's sort of complicated,' Jade said. 'You know what Nic's like. He's not the settling down type. This is a form of torture for him. He will want to shake off the shackles as soon as the time is up.'

'Is that what he told you?' Bronte asked, frowning slightly.

Jade looked across at Nic, who was now holding Bronte and Luca's baby boy, Marco, with Luca looking on indulgently. 'More or less,' she said, swinging her gaze back to Bronte's again. 'I'm not the right wife for him, Bronte. I don't know what Salvatore was thinking, writing his will the way he did. I could never make Nic happy. I don't have it in me to be a wife to anyone, let alone a man so restless and hard to please as him. I can't compete with supermodels and the like.'

Bronte gave her a gentle squeeze on the arm. 'I think you do yourself a very big disservice. You are one of the most beautiful women I have ever met, but not just in looks. I've seen the way you've cuddled Marco and Matteo, and I saw the way you tucked some of the flowers from your bouquet in Ella's hair. She already worships you. She thinks you're a princess. You *look* like a princess. I don't think I've ever seen a more stunning bride.'

'You're very kind,' Jade said, warming to the young woman all the more.

'I didn't get to know Salvatore very long, as you know,' Bronte said, 'but I knew enough about him to know he was no fool. If he thought the best course of action was to tie you and Nic in a marriage of convenience, then it would have been done out of love, not malice. He adored you. Luca has told me so many times of how he never had a bad word to say about you in spite of what the press reported over the years.'

Jade looked at the contents of her glass, swirling them around, just like the thoughts in her brain. 'How do you handle it?' she asked, looking up at Bronte again. 'The press, I mean. I'm pretty used to it but every now and again it gets to me. Do you find it hard after your life in Melbourne where you were anonymous for so long?'

Bronte's eyes went to her husband's and a smile spread over her features. 'After a while you forget about the press,' she said. 'It's about you and your husband. It's about building a family unit that is so strong it can withstand the intrusion of other forces.'

She turned her gaze back to Jade's. 'I understand how people are fascinated with celebrities. I was too to some degree, but now I realise we are all just normal people trying to do our best with the limited time we've got on this earth. You have to make the most of it. But I can tell you from experience that marrying into the Sabbatini family is a wonderful thing. I have never felt so loved and accepted, even though I still haven't quite mastered the language. Do you speak Italian?'

'I can understand it more than I can speak it. I'm pretty hopeless at languages,' she said and added wryly, 'I still have trouble with English.'

'It will be expected of you,' Bronte warned. 'Maya's been giving me lessons. I'm much better than I expected but, to tell you the truth, it's really rather embarrassing to be outdone by my little daughter.'

Nic came over at that point and slung a casual arm around Jade's shoulders. 'How are you holding up, *tesore mio*?' he asked.

'My face is aching from smiling so much,' she said truthfully.

'Don't worry,' he said. 'The party is almost over. Luca and Bronte's wedding went on for hours and hours, but then just as well, eh, Bronte?'

Bronte grinned as she looked to where Giorgio and Maya were cuddling up, no doubt remembering how they had come together for a stolen night of passion at Luca and Bronte's wedding whilst in the throes of an acrimonious divorce. 'You're not wrong there, Nic,' she said and discreetly slipped away when she heard Marco crying in the distance.

'Bronte thinks you would make a fabulous father,' Jade said, testing the waters with a bravado that had come from a few sips from a champagne glass.

Nic gave her a frowning look. 'Not me, baby girl. I like kids, I love them in fact, but I don't want any for myself. Children are hard work. They tie you down. I like my freedom too much.'

Jade felt an inexplicable ache deep inside her chest at his adamant statement. Surely she wasn't getting too attached to the loving wife role, not so soon? It was a role, an act. It wasn't for real. 'A lot of people would view that as a rather selfish stance to take,' she said, twirling her glass again for something to do with her hands.

His eyes narrowed as they centred on hers. 'Do *you* want children?' he asked.

Jade couldn't hold his gaze much longer than a second or two. 'Of course not,' she said, putting her glass down on the nearest surface. 'Having a child would totally cramp my lifestyle. You can't go clubbing with a baby, and just think what it would do to my figure.'

'So now who's the one who is being selfish?' he asked, hooking one brow upwards.

She looked up at him with a cool smile. 'I didn't say *I* thought it was a selfish decision; I just said a lot of people would take that view.'

He continued to look at her with unwavering intensity, as if he was measuring her words with her expression and finding something lacking. 'So no kids for both of us,' he said, rocking back on his heels as he thrust his hands in his trouser pockets. 'At least we both know the rules from the outset. I take it you're on the Pill?'

Jade raised her brows at him. 'That is hardly any of your business, considering this is not going to be a normal marriage.'

He smiled an indolent smile that crinkled up the corners of his hazel eyes. 'Still insisting on a hands-off arrangement, *cara*?' he said. He leaned in closer, right up against the shell of her ear, his warm breath skating over her flesh, making every nerve stand to attention. 'You might want to rethink that once all these guests leave. We will be all alone. Just you and me and a document saying we are legally married.'

Jade couldn't quite suppress the whole body shiver that consumed her. She stepped backwards and, scooping up her previously abandoned glass, took a hefty sip but, as far as boosting her courage, it did nothing but remind her of how terribly vulnerable she was and had always been when it came to Nic Sabbatini and his lethally sensual charm.

* * *

Finally it was over.

Jade stood with the band of Nic's strong arm around her waist as they farewelled their guests. It was a long, slow process as everyone wanted to express their congratulations and best wishes for a happy future. Jade felt at times that her smile was so forced it would crack her face in two.

It was far easier when it was just the family taking their leave before they were flown back to Milan. They, at least, all knew the terms of Salvatore's will, but even so Jade wondered if any of them, particularly Maya and Bronte, had any idea of the way she was feeling. The ambiguity of her feelings worried her. She had been determined to get Nic to marry her so she could have the financial security she longed for, but she hadn't factored in how being with him for extended periods would affect her. She felt it now, a slight tug in her insides every time he looked at her. A twist inside her stomach, a flutter inside her heart, a breathlessness in her chest, an ache deep in her core.

Giovanna, her new mother-in-law, was tearful,

but Jade knew that was more to do with having come back to the villa for the first time since baby Chiara had died all those years ago. Giovanna kissed Jade on both cheeks and welcomed her again to the family. 'I know this is not what either of you want, but do try and make the best of it, Jade. Our marriage had a rough start but I had many happy years with my Giancarlo.'

'I am sure we will make the best of things,' Jade assured her with zero confidence.

'Of all my boys, Nic is most like his father,' Giovanna said. 'He is restless, a free spirit—is that how you say it in English?'

'*Sì*, that is exactly how you say it,' Jade said.

Giovanna gave her another tight hug. 'You and Nic are more alike than you are different,' she said. 'Salvatore always said you were an angel underneath. That is just like my Nic. He has a soft core; you just have to know how to find it.'

Jade smiled wanly as the family escorted Giovanna to the waiting limousine. She was surprised at her new mother-in-law's attitude towards her. There were not many mothers who would welcome someone with Jade's reputation into the family, but then perhaps Giovanna was as eager as Salvatore had been for her youngest son to settle down, even if it wasn't to the most suitable of brides.

Nic came over to where Jade was standing, watching as the car disappeared into the distance. She felt her skin lift even though the air was still warm. She turned and faced him, forcing a stiff smile to her face. 'That seemed to go off rather well, don't you think?'

His eyes gleamed as he looked down at her. 'Everyone said the same thing: you were the most beautiful bride they have ever seen,' he said. 'I didn't tell you earlier, but you took my breath away when you stepped into the church on your father's arm.'

Jade didn't allow herself to believe he was being genuine. She knew what he wanted. He wanted to end the day in bed. He was a master at seduction and what better way than to butter her up with compliments that would melt her resolve to keep this marriage in name only. 'I think you went a little too far on the kiss in the church,' she said in a prim tone. 'A simple kiss on the lips would have sufficed. You should have shown a little more respect.'

His mouth tilted in a knowing smile. 'Feeling guilty about wanting me, Jade?'

She folded her arms across her middle. 'I do *not* want you. I just want the money this marriage will bring.'

'So you keep reminding me, but your eyes tell me something else again,' he said. 'And not just your eyes but your mouth as well. I've had trouble getting our first kiss out of my mind. You really are a little firecracker, aren't you?'

She gave a scathing little snort.

He studied her for a moment. 'Have you had anything to eat?'

She looked at him in irritation. 'Oh, please don't start on about that. I had enough from my father. Not that he was any great example, getting drunk like that and having to be practically poured into the car with his new girlfriend fussing over him as if she really gives a fig about him. She's after his money, any fool can see it, but then there's no fool like an old fool, is there?'

Nic pursed his lips for a moment. 'You don't really hate him, do you?'

She sent him a look that would have cut through marble. 'I feel nothing for him or for anyone.'

'I am quite sure that's not true,' he said. 'I saw you playing with Ella earlier. You don't hate her, do you?'

Her eyes flashed angrily. 'You seem to think you know me, Nic, but you don't. I'm not the naive, foolish, pampered little girl who hung off your every word like a lovesick puppy in the past. I've grown up. I know how to protect myself from people like you. You think you can throw a few compliments around and entice me into your bed, but I'm not that easy.'

'The press would have it otherwise,' he said with a wry look.

'The press don't always get it right,' she said. 'They interpret what they see to sell the most papers. It suits them to portray me as a home-wrecker. It fits their image of me as a tart who will bed anything in trousers. But I do have some standards. I am not interested in other people's husbands. I think that is the ultimate betrayal, to sleep with a close friend's husband.'

Nic studied her for another long moment, his thoughts flying around his head like insects trying to avoid the spurt of a poisonous spray. 'Are you saying the stuff about your affair with Richard McCormack was not true?'

She met his gaze with a challenge in her own. 'What do you think? Do you really think I am the sort of person to sleep with my best friend's husband while she was in the early stages of carrying his baby, which she subsequently lost?'

Nic raised his brows in surprise. There had been no mention of a baby in the press. He didn't know McCormack all that well personally, but they occasionally moved in the same circles. Nic had seen Richard at various functions, playing the role of the urbane businessman with consummate ease. He hadn't seemed the type to cheat on his wife, but then Jade was a temptation that would test any man's resolve. Nic felt it himself, the sensual power she had over him. Those sea-green eyes that promised so much, that lured and enticed, only to flash with hatred at the last minute. It was a cat and mouse game she was an expert at performing. But if she was innocent, then why not defend herself? She had access to top-notch lawyers. She wasn't exactly destitute, even if she had been a little overly dependent on her father's largesse up until now.

'So if you weren't McCormack's bit on the side, then who was?' he asked.

She gave him a stony-faced look. 'I have no idea.'

Nic wondered if she was lying to protect herself or someone else or whether she truly didn't know. It seemed the more time he spent with her, the less he knew about her. She had carried herself throughout the day so convincingly even he had to remind himself this was a temporary marriage, not the real thing at all. The way she had responded to his kiss, both in the church and the other day back at his villa in Rome, had revealed what a passionate woman she was under the surface of that cool don't-mess-with-me façade she customarily wore when around him. She wasn't immune to him any more than he was to her, although she insisted on denying it. Was it pride or part of the chase? He couldn't quite decide, but he was determined that he would make this marriage real, even if it took him the best part of the year to do it.

He smiled to himself as he thought of her soft full-lipped mouth around him, sucking on him, no doubt doing what she had done so many times with so many men. Oh, yes, she would come to him and come willingly. It was only a matter of time. He felt his body stirring to life, the blood rocketing through his veins as he thought of her writhing and twisting beneath him as he worked them both to the pinnacle of pleasure. A deep pool of longing started at the base of his spine and moved forwards, making him hard and ready for action.

'How about a drink to celebrate our temporary marriage?' he said, stretching an arm towards the villa.

She brushed past him with a glacial look. 'I have had my fill of celebratory drinks,' she said. 'I am going to bed.'

Nic paced the *salone* an hour or so later, wondering why he felt so restless and on edge. Actually, he did know why, it was just he didn't want to admit it. He had planned to have Jade in his bed by now and yet she had eluded him with a curt dismissal. He tossed back the contents of his glass, knowing it was probably unwise to overdo it but overdoing it anyway. What the hell was he doing spending his first night of married life—temporary as it was—alone with a brandy bottle?

He dragged a hand through his hair. This was ridiculous. He had to get a grip. Jade was not the woman he wanted to spend the rest of his life with. He didn't want to spend the rest of his life with any one woman. He wasn't like his brothers, who had settled down with their wives and children, content with their lot. He had always wanted more. More money, more excitement, more challenges.

He was unscrewing the bottle of brandy one more time when he heard a footfall on the stairs. He put the bottle back on the drinks counter and moved out to the hall. Jade was walking slowly down the stairs, step by step, her green eyes staring straight ahead, one of her hands sliding down the banister as if she was wary of falling head first.

'Jade?'

She totally ignored him. She continued on, step by soft step, her face expressionless. He blinked a couple of times, wondering if it was the brandy that had conjured her up, but no, she was still there, taking those ever so softly treading steps until she came to the base of the staircase. The nightgown she was wearing was sheer enough for him to see her slim naked form beneath it. His eyes feasted on those high perfect breasts, so full and round with those rosy-red nipples that he knew would be heaven to suckle on. He lowered his hungry gaze to the feminine cleft between her thighs and he imagined touching her there, filling her with his presence, making her feel him move inside her. It was all he could do not to go to her and pull her into his arms. He was about to take a step towards her when she looked around her with sightless eyes and sighed deeply before retracing her steps, all the way up the stairs again.

Nic watched, his throat rising and falling over a swallow as he realised she was sleepwalking. He considered waking her but then he recalled how he had read somewhere it was not the thing to do. You supposedly had to lead the person gently back to bed, to make sure they were safe.

He followed her up the stairs, keeping a few paces behind so as not to startle her. She padded back to the room she had chosen as her own. It was well away from the master suite, one of the spare rooms that in the past had been used for visitors. Half of her things were still waiting to be unpacked, in boxes and cases that littered the room. He made a mental note to get the housekeeper to sort it all out for her tomorrow.

He watched as Jade moved across the room and climbed back into the bed, pulling the sheet over her body and closing her eyes as her head came to rest on the pillow.

He stood watching her in the soft glow of the landing light for so long he lost track of time. After a while she made a murmuring sound and her lips fluttered over a deep sigh as she settled down even farther onto the pillow.

Nic took a scratchy breath and stepped closer to the bed. He reached out and gently brushed a strand of her dark, silky hair back off her face. She gave another soft little murmur, something unintelligible, but somehow it made him feel as if she instinctively trusted him. It gave him a strange feeling deep inside. He was the last person she should be trusting. 'Sweet dreams, *cara*,' he said and, before he could stop himself, he bent down and pressed a light as air kiss to her creamy, velvety cheek. Her lips twitched as if she was smiling in her sleep at the light caress.

Nic moved away from the bed and, with one last long look, he turned and walked out of the room and gently closed the door behind him.

CHAPTER SEVEN

JADE woke to the sound of a knock on the door. She scrambled upright and, hauling the sheets over herself, asked who was there.

'It's me, Nic.'

She felt her heart give a funny little start. 'Um…I'm not dressed.'

'I've seen it all, Jade,' he said with amusement colouring his tone. 'You've done nothing but flaunt it at me for the last week or so.'

She glowered at the door and then stiffened when it opened and Nic stepped in as if he owned the place. The fact that he did—or at least his family did—was beside the point. 'What do you think you are doing?' she said.

He came over carrying a tray with steaming hot tea and fresh rolls and a selection of home-made preserves. 'I thought you might like breakfast in bed,' he said. 'After all, you had a pretty restless night.'

Jade frowned and angled her head at him suspiciously. 'I...I did?'

He gave a nod as he set the tray down on the bed right next to her tightly clenched thighs. 'I found you sleepwalking at about two in the morning,' he said. 'Do you do that often?'

She felt her face colour up. 'How would I know?'

'Hasn't a previous lover found you wandering about like a ghost in the past?' he asked.

Jade rolled her lips together. She looked down at the curl of steam coming from the teapot on the tray, wondering if Nic, like her father, thought there was something wrong with her, something seriously wrong as inside her head. She had walked in her sleep at regular intervals in the first few months after her mother had died. Jon had usually found her wandering around the house and had gently led her back to bed. After he had been killed she had started again, only this time her father had wanted her to see someone about it. She had seen the disgust on his face, the disappointment that his only living child was defective in some way.

'Jade?' Nic tipped her face his way with the blunt tip of his index finger.

Jade felt the pulse of heat pass from his body to hers. It was like a slow burn on her skin, making it quiver with a longing she could not explain. 'No,' she said and sent her tongue out over her bone-dry lips. 'No one has ever mentioned it. I used to sleepwalk when I was a child. I thought I had stopped ages ago but it must have been the stress of the wedding and moving and so on.'

He exchanged his finger for his thumb on her chin, using it like a soft brush over the sensitive area just below her bottom lip. 'Sometimes I get the feeling you are not the person everyone thinks you are,' he said, his eyes holding hers as his thumb continued its mesmerising action.

Jade disguised a swallow. 'Wh…what makes you say that?' she asked, annoyed at the slight catch in her voice.

His eyes were more brown than green this

morning, reminding her of the shadows deep inside a forest. 'You have perfected your don't-mess-with-me-I-don't-give-a-damn air, but I think deep inside you are crying out for attention. You push everyone away but what you really want is someone to be close to, someone who understands you and accepts you as you are.'

Jade felt cornered. The tray containing the hot tea had her trapped on one side and she knew if she moved to the other it would spill and possibly burn Nic. 'I have no idea of what you are talking about,' she said, schooling her features into an expression of boredom.

He gave a slowly spreading smile and brushed the pad of his thumb over her bottom lip. It was like an electric shock as soon as his flesh touched hers; every nerve in her mouth leapt and tingled, eager for more. She wanted to send her tongue out again to taste where he had been but she fought the urge with an enormous effort. 'You play the glamorous socialite so well,' he said in a low, deep burr. 'You dress the part, you act the part, but there's something about you that doesn't quite fit.'

She tried to lift her chin but he captured it between his thumb and index finger as if he had anticipated her movement even before she had done so herself. 'Don't do that,' she said.

'You don't like it when I touch you like this?' he asked as he traced a slow-moving finger down the curve of her cheek.

Jade felt a responding quiver deep in her belly. 'I…um…n-no.'

'What about this?' he asked, leaning in and pressing a barely touching kiss to her left temple.

'N…no,' she croaked and then swallowed as he moved to her right temple. She felt a shiver pass through her, awakening every sense inside her body.

'What about here?' he asked and kissed the edge of her mouth, not on her lips but close enough for her to feel the masculine rasp of his unshaven skin.

Heat exploded inside her, blistering heat that

threatened to consume everything in its path, like her resistance and resolve, for instance. 'Don't do this to me, Nic,' she said in a breathless little voice that sounded nothing like her own. 'It will only make things so much harder in the end.'

His eyes lasered hers, holding them, searching them, as if he was looking for her soul in their depths. It seemed a very long time before he spoke. 'You're right,' he said, resettling the tray, which was threatening to slip off the bed. He stood upright and added, 'Have your breakfast. I have some work to see to, in any case.'

Jade blinked in a combination of surprise and disappointment. He could switch off his feelings just like that? She was still smouldering like hot coals while he was acting as if all of this was a game, a test to see how far he could go with her. She seethed as he strode nonchalantly out of the room. No doubt the business he had in mind had something to do with his mistress. He would probably be emailing or texting her within minutes and laughing about his loveless contract marriage and the money he stood to gain at the end of it. A year tied to a woman he had no respect for, no feelings for other than transient lust.

Jade pushed the untouched breakfast to one side as she got out of the bed. She had to remind herself that she had no choice but to put up with things as they were. She needed the money far more than Nic did. She could not survive without it. It wasn't as if she could go out and get a job. She had no skills, no qualifications and no experience.

The only thing she could do was paint, but who was going to pay her to do that when there were literally thousands of gifted art students selling their wares on the streets all over Europe? She had seen them in Milan the last time she had visited Salvatore before he'd died. A young man had sold her a beautiful watercolour of the Castillo. She had been generous to him, but how many people would do that for her? She had spent hours in galleries over the years, studying the masters and watching DVDs on their work, but none of it gave her the qualifications or indeed the confidence to feel a part of the art world. She felt like a fraud, a child dabbling in amongst gifted adults, pretending she had a chance to be like them. She didn't even have a proper studio. She had nowhere to set out her things so she could come and go as she pleased without having to pack everything up all the time.

She chewed at her lip as she looked out of the window of the villa. The lake was shimmering with the sunlight dancing on its surface in the distance. It was such a stunning view. She had been distracted by it so many times yesterday while she was supposed to be acting the role of the besotted bride. Her fingers had been twitching to get to her paints and brushes to capture the light on the water, or the way the roses in the garden hung from the terrace in a scented arras. Then there was the villa itself, so old and stately, so magnificently placed above the lake, set on five levels, with so many rooms surely there would be one she could use as a studio while they were here.

Jade quickly showered and dressed and, pulling her long hair back into a ponytail, she went on a tour of the villa. Even from her privileged background, she couldn't help being impressed by the villa's priceless artworks and sculptures. The marble floors were softened with Persian rugs and the antique furniture gave each room an old world charm that somehow was both stately and homely at the same time.

If there were any household staff around they were keeping themselves well in the background as Jade ran into no one while she was going from floor to floor and room to room.

She came to a room on the third level of the house that was clearly a nursery, but not a modern one. It was like stepping back in time as she walked through the threshold of the squeaky door. A shiver ran up her spine like a spider in a hurry as she looked about the room.

A teddy bear was leaning sideways in the cot. A jack-in-the-box was hanging over the edge of the mantelpiece where he had been released all those years ago and no one had thought to put him back inside ready for the next leap out. A doll with wide-open glassy eyes sat next to him, her pretty pink dress faded with the passage of time until it was almost but not quite white.

Over thirty years ago a baby girl called Chiara had been put to bed in that cot under the window and the next morning her oldest brother Giorgio had come in and found her lifeless.

Jade could feel the weight of grief close in on her. It was like a presence in the room. It reminded her of how her mother's room had felt when she had been told she was never coming home. Jade had gone in there repeatedly, just to check, just to see if everyone was wrong. She could still *smell* her mother's perfume. She had picked up her mother's lipstick tube and felt sure her mother would be back to reapply it as she so regularly did. Jade had felt her mother's presence as if she hadn't really been dead, but just waiting for the right time to come back. She had even dressed in her mother's clothes whenever she could until the day her father had ordered for them to be sent to a charity. It had taken years for her to accept her mother was not going to come back to her, years and years of quiet desperation until she had finally given up all hope.

Tears burned in her eyes as she went over to the cot. There was a soft pink blanket tucked in neatly, embroidered with little rosebuds. She trailed a fingertip over the fabric, wondering what that little girl would be like now if she had not died such an early tragic death. Would she be married with a baby or two of her own? Would she love her brothers as they clearly loved and supported each other? Would she have welcomed Jade to the family as graciously as everyone had, considering her tainted reputation?

'What are you doing?' Nic's voice spoke from the doorway.

Jade spun around, her heart leaping to her throat. 'I…I was just looking around…' she said lamely.

His eyes swept over the room, a mask settling over his face like a blind coming down over a window. 'This place needs to be cleaned out and redecorated. I've been telling my mother that for years.'

'Is that why you insisted on being married here?' Jade asked. 'To force her to face her grief?'

'Thirty-one years is a long time,' he said, glancing at the Tower of Pisa teddy bear before returning his gaze to hers. 'My mother never really recovered from the loss; I understand that part. No parent should lose a child; it's not the right order of things. That's why I understand what your father went through. But I felt it was time to move on. This place used to be our holiday home. I was too young to remember it, of course, but Giorgio and Luca said we spent every summer here. It seems such a waste to have it and not use it.'

'Why not sell it?'

'It's been in our family for generations,' he said. 'When Giorgio and Maya were going through their divorce she wanted to have it as part of the divorce settlement. Giorgio dug his heels in, however. There was no way any one of us would part with this place, not under any circumstances.'

Jade could see why, now she had toured most of the rooms and taken in the view from each of the windows. And then there was the fact that this was the last place their baby sister had smiled and chortled. It would be very hard to sell and move out after something as deeply personal and tragic as that. She wondered then if Nic's shallow take on life hid a deeper soul than he let on publicly. He lived life in the moment, but there was a side to him that suggested he was a lot more sensitive than most people realised. She wondered if the death of his sister had affected him more than he let on. He had been young, yes, but his parents would have been devastated by their grief. Perhaps Nic had been left to fend for himself during that tragic time. Small children picked up on even the most subtle of changes in a household, let alone something as tragic as the loss of a sibling. They could be affected in ways the experts were only just discovering now. The sense of abandonment at such a tender age could permanently change the architecture of a small child's brain. Had Nic shut off his feelings because there was no one there to listen to him, to be there for him? Who had cuddled and comforted him? His brothers would have been far too young to see to his emotional needs. Nic had been a toddler, younger than little Ella. It was so sad to think of him wandering about this huge villa with no one to take proper emotional care of him apart from nannies and servants.

'Why do you love this place so much if you were too young to even remember it?' she asked.

His expression was still shuttered. 'I am not as sentimental about it as my brothers are but I still don't think it should be left empty for most of the year.'

'How do you think your mother coped with coming back here after all this time?' she asked.

His broad shoulders rose and fell in a shrug. 'She was emotional, as you saw, but then my mother has always been that way. She coped pretty well, I think. She came up here to the nursery with Maya. Maya said she thought it was a major turning point for *Mamma*. She needed to come back, to say a proper goodbye. She didn't get the chance at the time. It all happened so suddenly. It was so different back then. There wasn't much information on Sudden Infant Death Syndrome. For years my mother blamed herself. I think she thought everyone else blamed her too.'

'Is that why you don't want to have children?' Jade asked.

His expression tightened, as if pulled inward by invisible strings. 'No, Jade, I am just selfish, like you said. I value my freedom too much. This marriage is a means to an end. Don't get any ideas of making it anything it was never meant to be.'

Jade opened her mouth to respond but, before a single word could come out, he had turned and left her with the silent ghosts of the past...

When Jade came downstairs later that evening she found Nic in the *salone*, pouring himself a drink. He turned when he heard her come in and held up the bottle he was holding. 'Would you care to join me in a drink?' he asked.

Jade agreed to have a very weak white wine spritzer and sat on the edge of one of the sumptuous sofas, holding the frosted glass in her hands once he had fixed it for her.

'So,' he said, looking down at her with a mocking smile lurking about his mouth. 'Here we are then. Our second day of marriage is almost over. Only three hundred and sixty-three to go.'

She returned his look with a little hoist of her chin. 'You're not the only one counting the days, Nic.'

'I know of a very good way to pass the time,' he said with a dark glint in his eyes.

Jade felt a frisson of excitement rush through her in spite of her determination to keep things cool and impersonal between them. All day long she had lived with the expectation of running into him while she moved about the villa and its grounds. Every corner she turned, every door she opened and every corridor she traversed, she had felt a flicker of heady expectation that at some point Nic would track her down. Why he hadn't both intrigued and irritated her. 'I am sure you are very practised in spending time in pointless liaisons,' she said. 'How is your mistress taking the news of your marriage, by the way?'

He took a deep sip of his drink before he answered. 'She was coming up to her use-by date, in any case. I have no time for clingy, needy women. They bore me senseless.'

Jade felt as if a dagger had just pinned her heart to her backbone. She would stand no chance with him if he knew even half of the needs and insecurities she had. That she even wanted a chance with him showed how vulnerable she had become. A few days ago she had hated him with a vengeance… Now she was not so sure. 'I hope you're not expecting me to take over where she left off,' she said, keeping her voice steady and controlled with an effort.

His cynical smile said it all. 'I think you know what I want, Jade. You want it too, but for some reason you are holding out on me. What do you want? More money than you are already getting?'

Her mouth tensed as she threw him a cutting look. 'Is that how you charmed all those women into your bed, by dangling huge sums of money in front of them?'

He came up close, taking her glass out of her trembling hand before she could do anything to stop him. He drew her to her feet, her body so close to his she could feel his warmth. 'Why don't I show you how I do it?' he asked as he pressed a soft feather of a kiss to the side of her mouth.

Jade could feel her body swaying towards him. She tried to counteract the urge but it was as if her body was operating independently of her reason. A shiver fluttered like soft wings beating all the way down her spine, and her breasts tightened in heightened awareness of his warm hard chest pressed against them. She felt the stirring of his erection and for a moment had to fight not to pull away. This was not some faceless man she had been flirting with, teasing and acting out to show the world how tough she was. This was Nic; this was the one man she had always wanted.

It was Nic Sabbatini, her husband for the next twelve months.

He put a hand to the small of her back and pressed her against him, his breath a caress over her lips, which were aching for his kiss. 'You are driving me crazy with those looks you keep giving me. Are you doing it deliberately to make me beg?'

Jade ran the tip of her tongue out over her lips, her eyes going to his mouth—so close, so temptingly close. 'I'm trying to be sensible about this…'

'Forget being sensible,' he growled just above her mouth. 'Nothing about this arrangement is sensible, in any case.'

Jade wasn't sure if he came down or she rose up to meet his mouth in an explosively hot kiss. She didn't really care. All she knew was her body was on fire for him as soon as their lips came into full contact. His tongue probed for entry and she gave a little gasp of longing, a space inside her stomach hollowing out as he stroked and teased her tongue into seductive play with his. His kiss was slow and sensual one minute and determined and daring the next. Jade felt the simmering of her blood as his teeth gently nipped at her bottom lip in little tease and tug bites that triggered something deeply primal inside her.

His mouth moved from hers to burn across the sensitive skin of her neck and décolletage in a slow-moving journey that made every cell of her body cry out for more. She felt the liquid honey of desire between her thighs and the aching of her tight nipples where they were pressed so firmly up against his chest. The hand that had rested in the small of her back had now moved to boldly cup her bottom; the other hand was already seeking the soft swell of her right breast. She could scarcely believe the way her body responded to his touch, even though it was through the barrier of her clothes. Tremors of reaction ricocheted through her, making her ache to be naked with him, to feel him skin on skin, hot flesh on hot flesh. She placed her arms around his neck, letting her fingers delve into the thickness of his hair, relishing in the way he felt to her touch.

'*Dio*, I want you so badly,' Nic said against her mouth. 'But then you are a witch at making men want you, are you not? A seductive little witch with a mouth of fire.'

Jade ignored his comment to concentrate on the magical feeling of being so aware of her body, so in touch with its every need. Like how wonderful it felt to have his hand move under her top to cup her through the lace of her bra. The possessive press of his palm was mind-blowing; so too was the slow but sure stroke of his thumb against her engorged nipple. For all his intentions to get her into his bed, he was certainly taking his time about it, she thought as his mouth sucked on her nipple right through the lace of her bra. If anything, it intensified the sensation of his lips and tongue, making her almost mad with longing.

She arched her head back to give him better access, her body quivering inside and out as he kissed his way back up from her breast to her mouth. His masterful tongue this time was even more determined to conquer hers. He swept every corner of her mouth, exploring her, tasting her, tempting her into a dance of desire that she suspected could only end one way. She felt the ripples of it beginning deep and low in her body, the stirring of her senses so intense she was unable to think of anything but how he made her feel.

He tore his mouth off hers, his breathing hectic and his hazel eyes dark as they meshed with hers. 'Not here. Not like this,' he said, scooping her up into his arms and carrying her out of the *salone* towards the stairs. 'I want you in bed with me where you belong.'

Jade knew she should have called a halt right there and then. It was a chance to break the spell, a moment to reorient herself, to remind herself of his motives and her shameful secret. But somehow she couldn't do it. She wanted to feel his arms around her, to feel all that it was possible to feel when you truly wanted someone and they wanted you because they felt so in tune with you physically.

The master bedroom was a suite of massive

proportions but Jade was barely aware of her surroundings once Nic placed her on the big bed and came down beside her. He kissed her again, a slow searing kiss that made the blood race all over again in her veins. He had such a beautiful mouth, so firm and yet so sensually soft, as if she was the most precious fragile person he had ever kissed. He tasted so nice too, not of stale smoke and alcohol but a taste she would forever associate with him: essential maleness in its prime.

While his mouth continued to cast its spellbinding magic on hers, she felt his hands start to work on her clothes. She lifted her arms above her head as he peeled her top away. And then she raised her hips when he eased her out of her jeans, barely registering the soft thud of her shoes as they landed on the floor. She had been naked with a few men but she had never wanted to look at them the way she wanted to look at Nic. Her fingers set to work on his shirt and then, when that was cast aside, she worked on the waistband of his trousers, sliding down the zip, her breath stalling in her throat as she saw the way he had tented his underwear. She ran an experimental finger down the length of him through the fabric and watched as he quivered in response.

'Careful, *cara*,' he said in a gravelly tone. 'I want to last long enough to pleasure you.'

Her own pleasure had never been a priority before now. She had always pretended, giving her few past partners what she thought they had wanted. It had been easy and she had felt no guilt or remorse about it. But now she felt as if everything had changed. She wanted to give and receive pleasure because with Nic she knew it would be something completely different, something special, something to remember for the rest of her life once he moved on, as she was certain he would do.

Jade peeled back his underwear and stroked him again, her belly tightening in anticipation. She circled him with her fingers and saw his stomach muscles clench as she began moving up and down.

He pulled her hand away and pushed her back

down on the bed. 'Later,' he said and reached for the nearest bedside drawer for a condom.

She watched as he put it on, her breath hitching in her throat as she thought of him filling her. A flicker of nervousness passed through her. What if she wasn't able to please him? That had never been an issue with anyone else. She had given them what they wanted while her mind went elsewhere. But what if Nic saw through her pretence?

It seemed ridiculous to admit it, but this felt as if she was starting all over again. Each touch of his fingers was a new experience; it had nothing to do with her wretched, sordid past—it was as if that had happened to someone else, not her. His gentle caressing of her with his clever fingers was like an act of worship; it was not in any way exploitative or crude. He was stroking her into a whirlpool of sensation she had never experienced. She could feel her body climbing a mountain so high and spectacular it took her breath away.

'You're so beautiful and feminine I want to taste you,' he said in a husky voice.

No one had ever touched her quite like this, with such reverence, such tenderness and concern for her needs. She felt the movement of his lips against her and then the soft brush stroke of his tongue, once, twice, three times and then with an increase in pace. It was so raw, so intimate and so deeply erotic she felt her body gather all its energy at one point. A delicious tension began to pull at her, making her rise on a wave that felt so precipitous she wondered if she was going to crash and burn if—or when—she fell off.

'Come for me, *cara*,' he said in between caresses. 'I want to watch you lose yourself totally in what I am doing to you.'

Jade felt a bubble of emotion come up in her chest. She was unprepared for the way she was feeling, for how her body was reacting. But then, before she could examine her emotional response any further, the pinnacle of pleasure sneaked up on her, catching her totally off guard, making her spiral into a vortex of intensely pleasurable sensations that made her mind empty of everything but what she was feeling physically.

When the waves of pleasure finally subsided she felt hot, stinging tears come to her eyes. She put a hand up to hide them, to force them back, to do anything to stop them from betraying her, but it was too late.

Nic had already propped himself up on his arms, his frowning gaze going straight to hers. 'What's going on?' he asked.

Jade bit her lip to try and stop herself from bawling like a child. 'Nothing—sorry about this...' She swiped at her streaming eyes with the back of her hand. 'I'm not used to being so emotional when...I mean during...sex...'

He blotted another trail of tears with the pad of his thumb. 'Do you want to tell me what's so different about this time?' he asked gently.

Jade pressed her trembling lips together but she had no control over the sobs that seemed to be coming up from deep inside her. There was nothing she could do to hold the rushing, gushing emotions back. She shook her head and covered her eyes with both of her hands, a choked sob escaping as she gulped, 'Sorry about this…I'll be OK in a minute…just give me a minute…'

Nic peeled her hands away from her face, his gaze serious and concerned as he looked into her eyes. '*Cara*, did I do something you didn't like? Did I hurt you in some way?'

She shook her head and bit down on her bottom lip, fighting to rein in her runaway emotions. 'No, of course you didn't hurt me—it's just that…that I've never…it's just that it's never been like that before…'

His frown made a map of lines come up on his forehead. 'Are you saying you've never had an orgasm through oral sex before?'

Jade couldn't hold his penetrating look. She lowered her gaze to his throat, where she could see a pulse beating like a drum. She took a breath that felt rough around the edges and said, 'I've never had an orgasm before. Period.'

His throat moved up and down like a piston. Seconds passed, maybe only one or two but it felt like a month of them to her. 'I'm not sure I understand,' he said, bringing her chin up so her gaze met his. 'You're not a virgin, *sì*?'

Jade gave him a pained wry look. 'No, Nic, I am not a virgin.'

He moved his mouth a couple of times, as if searching for the right words to say. 'So, what I think you're saying is sex has not always been pleasurable for you, is that it?'

She let out a heavy sigh and shook her head as she dropped back on the pillow.

He gently brushed back some tendrils of her hair off her face, his touch so soft it made Jade feel another wave of emotion rise to the surface. 'Do you want to tell me about it?' he asked.

Jade looked into his hazel eyes, so very dark and serious as they held hers. Most men would have continued on to get their measure of pleasure out of her body by now, but he had not. It surprised her, given his playboy reputation. 'Don't you want to finish this?' she asked, waving her hand to encompass their bodies lying so close to each other.

He frowned even more darkly and got off the

bed, pulling off the condom and tossing it to one side. He reached for his trousers and pulled them on and zipped them. 'I am not sure what sort of man you think I am, Jade, but there's no way I am going to make love with you unless I know everything, and I mean everything.'

Jade tugged at the top sheet and pulled it over herself to cover her nakedness. Shyness was not normally an issue with her, she had grown so used to disconnecting her mind from her body, but somehow with Nic it was different. She felt exposed in a way she had never felt with anyone else. Nic saw things she wasn't sure she wanted him to see.

'Why don't you start at the beginning?' he suggested.

She gave him a mutinous look as she hugged her knees close to her body. 'I don't have to tell you anything. I wish I hadn't told you what I did. You're making such a big deal out of it.'

'Damn it, Jade, this *is* a big deal,' he said, shoving a hand through his already mussed-up hair. 'You can't drop a bomb like that into the bedroom and expect me to carry on as if nothing's changed.'

She couldn't hold his gaze and dropped her chin to rest on the tops of her bent knees. This wasn't supposed to happen. This was too personal, too invasive. She had tried to be so strong. With any other man she would have pulled it off, but not with Nic. He was her nemesis. She had always suspected it was the case. He would totally unravel her, leaving her vulnerable and exposed.

'Tell me, Jade,' he said, his voice lowering to a gentle burr. 'Tell me why it is that with the kind of reputation you have—which, I might add, you have not in any way discouraged or taken any action to defend yourself—you have not until this point enjoyed sex fully.'

Jade slowly lifted her head off her knees. It seemed she was not going to get out of this after all. She knew Nic well enough to know he would stand there and wait for her to tell him, no matter how long it took. It was her fault for letting him get under her radar. She should have known he would be the one to see through her party-girl pretence. Shame coursed through her but she made herself meet his dark gaze. 'Do you remember the night of my sixteenth birthday when I tried to seduce you?' she asked.

He nodded grimly. 'It's not something I like to think about too much. I tried to do the right thing by you. I know I was a little hard on you. I've often thought if I had handled it better you might not have rushed off with Riccardo.'

Jade got off the bed, dragging the sheet with her as a drape. She wanted her clothes on but dressing in front of him was out of the question. She felt far too exposed as it was.

'Here,' Nic said, handing her his bathrobe from the back of the door to the en suite bathroom. 'Put this on.'

Jade slid her arms into the sleeves and tied the ends around her waist. It was far too big for her; she felt as if she were wrapped in a circus tent.

'You look like Ella playing dress-ups with her mother's clothes.'

She gave him her version of a smile: sad and wistful. 'I wish I could go back to her age and start again. Maybe I wouldn't make the same mistakes.'

His brow tightened again with a frown. 'We all make mistakes, Jade. It's what life is about: living and learning. We can't grow until we realise where we went wrong.'

She hugged her arms close to her body. 'I should have listened to you that night,' she said, no longer able to meet his eyes. 'I should have taken on board everything you said. But I didn't. Instead, I did the very opposite. I was so rebellious, so determined to show you and everyone I could do what I wanted. But I was wrong—so terribly, terribly wrong.'

Nic felt a tremor of unease pass through his insides. This was a side to Jade he had never seen before: the vulnerable side. Gone was the tough don't-mess-with-me-I-couldn't-give-a-damn-anyway wild-child; in her place was a young woman who looked as if the world had let her down in a very bad way. He didn't say anything. He kept silent to let her continue, but he felt his throat tighten as he swallowed, as if a rough hand had grasped him by the neck and squeezed until he could hardly breathe.

She looked up at him, her forest-green eyes filled with pain. 'Sleeping with your friend is something I have always regretted. It was nothing like I thought it would be. I wanted to get back at you for rejecting me, but instead I was the one who got hurt.'

The hand around Nic's neck tightened another notch. 'Did that bastard hurt you?' he asked.

She tugged at her bottom lip with her teeth for a moment before answering. 'No, at least not by intention. You were right, Nic; I was too young to be having sex. I wasn't ready emotionally. I allowed someone I hardly knew to use my body. I was so ashamed when it was over. I cried for hours. But then, instead of learning from my mistake, I did it again. I was suddenly popular. I was the IT girl when for so long I was the one on the outside. I suppose it was a way to get attention.'

Nic momentarily closed his eyes. He opened them to find her looking into the distance, as if she were time travelling to the past. 'Jade…' he began and took a step towards her but she held up her hand like a stop sign.

'No,' she said. 'Let me get this off my chest. God knows, it's about time.' She gave a harsh-sounding laugh that contained no humour in it at all. 'For all these years I have pretended to live like a tart. I let the press portray me like that. I actively sought that sort of reputation by being in all the hip places, dressing provocatively, flirting, teasing, acting as if I was the most popular girl in town. I guess that's the way I saw myself: the cheap, shallow socialite, the reckless, uncontrollable wild-child who didn't give a damn what anyone thought about her.'

'But you do care about what people think of you, don't you, Jade?' Nic said. 'Your father, for instance. For all these years you've been acting out to get his attention, but it hasn't worked, has it?'

She gave him another world-weary twist of her lips. 'He's never quite forgiven me for not going on that holiday. If I had been with Jon he wouldn't have gone to that particular ski run. Jon was always my father's favourite. I knew that. Jon knew that, but he tried his best to compensate by being the best brother you could imagine. Without him, I was like a rudderless boat. I couldn't seem to stop from hitting the rocks. It was like I was determined to self-destruct or something.'

'You are not to blame for your brother's death,' he said. 'There is no way you should be blamed by anyone for that, especially your father.'

'I can't turn back the clock,' Jade said sadly. 'I wish I could, not just with that holiday but everything really. I wish I had had more time with my mother. I think I would have fared better if she hadn't died when she did. She would have helped me with my—' She stopped and bit her lip again.

'Helped you with your what, Jade?' he prompted.

She met his gaze. 'Um…with my art work.'

He frowned. 'Your art work?'

Jade felt her face grow warm. 'Yes, I sort of dabble in watercolours. I'm not very good. I haven't taken any lessons or anything. It's just a hobby. Actually, I'm totally rubbish at it. I would never show anyone my stuff. It just fills in the time for me. I enjoy it, you know, the creative part of it.'

'I am sure you are being unnecessarily harsh on your talent.'

'I have no qualifications,' she said. 'Not unless you count hours, if not days, wandering around galleries and art shows. I just know what I like and what I like to paint. That's all, really. I don't even have a proper studio.'

He looked at her for a long moment. 'Would you like to have a studio of your own?'

Jade felt a frisson of creative excitement rush through her. She also felt a flutter of something deep inside her heart—a feeling of gratitude that he hadn't laughed at her or ridiculed her painting but instead was offering his support. 'Do you think I could use one of the rooms in your villa in Rome as a studio?' she asked tentatively. 'I've brought some stuff with me here but we won't be here long enough for me to set up properly.'

'Use whatever room suits you, both here and in Rome. Do you need anything? Art supplies and so on?'

'No, I have everything I need,' she said. 'I packed it all when I left London.'

He looked at her in silence for another moment or two. 'You really are full of surprises, aren't you, *cara*?' he said.

Jade felt the warm glow on her cheeks intensify and quickly lowered her eyes. 'We all have our secrets, I suppose.'

'What you see is what you get with me, I'm afraid,' he said with a wry smile. 'Shallow and selfish is what the press call me, isn't it? And, let me tell you, it's not far off the truth.'

Jade meshed her gaze with his. 'I don't believe that.'

He raised his brows at her. 'You don't?'

She shook her head. 'You are a lot deeper than you allow people to think. Sensitive too, much more sensitive than people give you credit for.'

He gave her a guarded look. 'What makes you say that?'

She kept her eyes trained on his. 'You are not like the other men I know or have known in the past. I've always felt like that about you. You stand apart from everyone.'

A flash of something moved across his features. 'Listen, Jade,' he said. 'Don't go getting any ideas about me settling down and playing happy husband for ever. This is the shallow, selfish part of me I warned you about talking here, and it's the real me. This marriage is solely to access my share of my grandfather's estate. It is not about building a future together or falling in love. Are we both clear on that?'

Jade schooled her expression into blankness, but inside she felt the pain of rejection eat away at her like sharp little teeth. It was like all those years ago, but worse somehow. She wasn't good enough for him. She was never going to be good enough for him. Telling him why she had acted the way she had had made it worse, not better. He was sympathetic and supportive and she was grateful for that, but she was fooling herself if she thought such a heart-to-heart confession was going to make him fall in love with her. He was not interested in settling down, and certainly not with someone who had acted with such impropriety for as long as he had known her.

'Jade?' He pushed up her chin with his finger.

She jerked her head away and got to her feet. 'What do you take me for, Nic?' she asked. 'I told you before, I'm not some naive schoolgirl with a crush. So we had sex, or at least you pleasured me. Thanks, by the way. It was great. Very memorable, but it doesn't mean I have feelings for you.'

He watched her for a beat or two before he responded. 'Just keep a lid on it, that's all I'm saying, Jade. I know what happens when women find a lover who finally ticks all the boxes for them. The lines get blurred. Sex for me is a physical thing. I love it, not necessarily the person I am having it with.'

Jade folded her arms across her body. 'I'm not going to fall in love with you, Nic.' *Because a part of me has already gone ahead and foolishly and irrevocably done so*, she thought in silent despair.

He walked to the bedroom door but stopped and turned around to look at her before he opened it. 'The money is not just for me,' he said. 'If I lost my share of the Sabbatini Corporation it might have put my brothers at risk of a one-third takeover. These have been pretty rough financial times in recent years. It is not sound business sense to be off your watch, even for a moment. My grandfather knew that and used it to get me to do what he wanted. He had a fantasy about you and me making a match of it, but that's all it was: a fantasy. None of this is real, Jade. It's like acting a role in a play. Our primary job is to get through this year and collect our earnings at the end.'

Jade lifted one of her finely arched brows. 'Does that mean you will no longer require my services in bed? I too can separate the act from the emotion. I've been doing it all these years. I am happy to oblige. After all, I owe you one, Italian boy.'

He frowned at her choice of words. 'Don't play the cheap tart with me, Jade. It doesn't suit you.'

She threw him a what-would-you-know look, but he had already gone.

CHAPTER EIGHT

JADE didn't bother leaving the comfort of Nic's bed, even though she was uncertain of what he expected of her now. Their relationship had stepped to a new level, but it wasn't quite where she wanted it to be. Sharing a room and a bed was not going to be enough for her. She knew it would break her heart the longer it continued, but right now she couldn't bring herself to leave the sheets that smelled of him. Her body was still tingling from the earth-shattering experience of his touch and caresses. She squeezed her thighs together, marvelling at the way her inner body still pulsed and ached for more of that delicious pleasure.

She must have drifted off to sleep for suddenly she heard the door of the bedroom open and Nic came in with a wry expression on his face. 'I thought you might have bolted to the room down the hall by now,' he said.

She sat up and hugged her knees and glared at him. 'I was seriously thinking about it.'

His mouth slanted in a smile. 'But here you are, waiting for me.'

She narrowed her eyes. 'I'm not waiting. I fell asleep.'

He moved closer to the bed, his hazel eyes dark as a shadowed swamp as they ran over her. 'Move over, *cara.*'

Jade's eyes flared, along with her desire. It was like an exotic flower opening inside her, the soft petals unfurling against the walls of her femininity, tickling her, reminding her of what it would feel like to have him there, moving intimately inside her. 'Since when am I supposed to take orders from you?' she asked with an attempt at her usual brash bravado, which somehow this time didn't quite make the grade.

Nic smiled and dropped his bathrobe. 'If you don't move I will have to move you and who knows what might happen then, hmm?'

Jade smoothed the crumpled sheets for something to do with her hands rather than putting them where she most wanted to put them. She didn't want to appear desperate and clingy and needy, but, dear God, how good it was to look at him. He smelt divine: male musk and citrus rolled up in a delicious aroma that was like an irresistible drug. His body was already responding. She tried not to look but how could she not? She ached deep inside for his body to show her what she had been missing for all this time.

Nic cupped her cheek and trained his gaze on hers. 'There you go again, giving me that look. For the last couple of hours downstairs I told myself I was going to take my time, let you feel your way with me a bit. But how am I supposed to resist you when you look at me like that?'

'How am I looking at you?' she asked, licking her lips, which were dryer than paper.

He groaned and joined her on the bed, his head coming down as hers lifted up for his kiss. Their tongues met in a sexy duel, hot, moist and hungry. It went on and on, fuelling Jade's need with each throbbing second. She felt her body ripen in awareness, the way her breasts ached and the way her feet arched in pleasure each time he deepened the kiss. Her belly was a deep, bottomless pool of longing, her limbs like jungle vines that wrapped around him to hold him to her. Her hips were beneath the blessed weight of his, the pressure of his erection an erotic reminder of what she had yet to experience with him.

He took his mouth off hers to work his way down to her breasts, taking his time, drawing out her pleasure until she could barely think. That first suckle of his mouth on her nipple made her back come right off the bed, and her arms tightened their hold on him. He flicked his tongue back and forth and then around and around until she was like molten wax, limbless and boneless, her head spinning with the impact of such new sensations.

'You taste so divine,' he said against the cup of her shoulder as he worked his way back up to her mouth. 'Orange blossom and honeysuckle with a touch of vanilla.'

'You taste good too,' she said, surprised her voice could even function while her senses were in such overload. She stroked her tongue over his bottom lip, teasing him, waiting to see what he did.

His eyes became hooded as he gazed at her mouth, his tongue moving out over his lips to moisten them before he swooped down and covered hers. The pressure increased as his passion intensified, but Jade still felt as if he was holding back. She decided to take matters into her own hands and sent them to work on his body: touching him, exploring him in exquisite detail. He groaned under her handiwork, his breathing becoming all the more ragged the more daring she became. It was liberating for her to touch him when and how she wanted, to feel the satin of his skin, to feel the steely length of him quivering in the circle of her fingers. She kissed her way down from his mouth, all the way down his chest, dipping the tip of her tongue into the shallow pool of his belly button, watching as the ridged muscles of his abdomen contracted in anticipation of the rest of the journey.

He put a hand on the back of her head, gently grasping a handful of her hair to stop her.

Jade felt a rush of feminine power she had never felt before. This time it wasn't about privately sneering at the selfish lack of control some men had, it was about her effect on Nic and how he felt under her touch. He wasn't the sort of man to lose control. He was a playboy who had had numerous lovers before, but for some reason with her he was having trouble keeping his head. She backed off and waited for him to regulate his breathing, watching him, enjoying every flicker of emotion that passed over his face.

He brushed her mouth with his and then touched down again, lingering this time in a kiss that went on and on. His hands slid down her body and she relished the feel of his palms and fingers on her naked flesh. She didn't send her mind away; instead, she felt herself blooming under his touch. She moved against his pelvis, seeking his hardness, her body achingly empty, hot and moist and ready for him.

He touched her with his fingers, playing with her, ramping up her need until she was writhing beneath him, breathlessly begging for him to take her to paradise as he had before.

'Please, Nic, don't make me wait any longer, please.'

He made a sound deep in his throat and reached across her for a condom. This time she took it from him and rolled it over him, watching as his body burgeoned with the need to explode. 'You are making this so hard for me to slow down,' he said against her mouth. 'I want this to be special for you. I don't want to rush you.'

She cupped his unshaven face with her hands, every nerve in her palm responding to his raspy maleness. 'I want you, Nic, like I have never wanted anyone else. I feel like I have been waiting all of my life for this moment.'

'Me too,' he said, almost too low for her to hear as he nudged against her slick entrance.

Jade felt the shockwave of delight rush like

a river through her. It felt so good to have him against her sensitive flesh; the feel of his strength against her softness was pure bliss. She pushed up with her hips and he surged into her, his attempt to check himself lost as her body gripped him tightly, taking him fully. He groaned again as he was catapulted into the vortex of passion that had already swept her away on its rapid tide. She felt the ripples of pleasure roll through her body from head to foot. Tension built and built, spiralling upwards as she climbed to the summit with him in fast pursuit. Suddenly she was crying out at the sheer magnitude of it as it smashed against her like a giant wave. She was tossed about, rolled over and over until she was a limbless, mindless rag doll, limp with satiation in his arms.

She was conscious enough to feel his orgasm fire like a bullet out of a barrel. She felt his flesh pucker in goose bumps where her hands slid along his back, his skin slick with perspiration, a sexy humid heat that she wanted to bask in for ever.

Jade had never felt comfortable with the after sex chit-chat routine. She had never quite worked out what the right thing to say was when it was over, so she usually said nothing. But this was different.

Way, way different.

She wanted to cuddle up close and feel Nic's heart beating next to hers. She wanted to breathe in his scent, to commit it to memory for the time when he would no longer be in her life. She wanted to hold him within her until he grew hard again. When it came down to basics, she just didn't want it to be over.

Not yet.

Not ever.

Nic moved away and pulled the condom off but Jade noticed he was frowning.

'Is something wrong?' she asked and sat upright but then she felt what he was frowning about.

'The condom didn't do its job. There must have been a tear in it or something.'

Jade looked at him with wide eyes. 'Oh…'

He raked a hand through his hair. 'You're on

the Pill, right? You said you were on the Pill. It should be fine. I don't have anything. I have regular checkups. I'm totally safe; are you?'

She didn't speak. Her mind was running ahead with the image of a baby—a gorgeous dark-haired baby. She gave herself a mental shake. Having a baby with Nic would not make him love her nor would it be right in a temporary marriage. And what sort of mother would she make, in any case?

'Jade?'

She moved away so he wouldn't see the longing in her eyes. 'Of course I'm safe,' she said, doing what she had to do with the tissues with as much dignity as the circumstances allowed. 'I've been taking the Pill since I was sixteen.'

'Fine, then,' he said, sounding immensely relieved. 'We could probably forgo condoms from now on if we both are exclusive.'

Jade kept her back turned to him. *Exclusive?* He was intending to sleep with only her for the next few months? Hope flared like a beacon in her chest but she quickly doused it.

'Can I trust you on that?' she said, finally turning to meet his gaze.

'When I give my word, I mean it,' he said. 'You should know that about me, Jade.'

The air hummed with a singing wire of escalating want.

'Come here,' Nic said, sending a shiver of reaction to her toes and back.

Jade slowly turned around, the task of getting back into her bathrobe somehow losing its importance as she met his burning gaze. 'You…you want me?'

His hands cupped her shoulders as she stepped towards him. 'I have always wanted you, Jade,' he said and brought his searing mouth down to hers.

For the next week, while they stayed at the villa, Nic took her on a sensual journey that was beyond exciting and exhilarating. He introduced her to the delights of the flesh that made her tingle all over when she thought about all they experienced together. They had made love in the shower, in the moonlight, on the deck by the pool, in the gardens with the scent of roses heavy in the air. He had been gentle but passionate with her, urging her into new and even more exciting territory, not stopping until she was blissfully satisfied before he took his own pleasure. It had made her realise how different sex was in the context of a relationship, how it intensified every touch and stroke, or at least it did for her. She could only assume Nic was unaffected, other than physically. He enjoyed sex; he was, after all, a very physically fit man in the prime of his life. He had energy to burn and she willingly partnered him in marathon sessions that left her quivering and tingling for hours afterwards. It was difficult not to think of all the other women he had pleasured before her, but then she reminded herself that she was no plaster saint and, while her experience was nothing to be proud of, she often wondered if he thought of the men she had slept with and felt any stirring of jealousy.

One of the things that had most touched her during that week was Nic's insistence on seeing some of her art work. He refused to take no for an answer, and so she found herself opening the door of the room she had commandeered on the top floor of the villa. She had unpacked the few materials she had brought with her and made a makeshift easel by using books propped up on a desk to make the most of the light. The water-colour she was working on was a scene from the villa gardens where a fountain was surrounded by clipped low-lying hedges, and in the background was the sparkling blue of the lake and the mountains beyond. It wasn't her best work and she felt uncomfortable showing him it half-done but he seemed totally entranced as he looked at it.

'You did this?' he said, turning from the painting to look at her.

Jade gave a self-conscious nod. 'I know it's not terribly professional. I haven't been to art school or anything. I'm just an amateur, as I told you.'

'May I?' Nic asked as he pointed to the little stack of unframed paintings she had brought with her.

She felt her face heating with embarrassment

and silently prayed he wouldn't laugh at her paltry attempts to capture a favourite scene. 'Go ahead,' she said. 'But they're not worth anything. They're not even worth framing.'

He went through the paintings one by one, looking in detail at each brush stroke and nuance of light and colour.

Jade stood, awkwardly shifting her weight from foot to foot, feeling like the times she had waited for her father's verdict on yet another wretched school report.

'Jade, these are amazing,' Nic said, breaking through her thoughts. His eyes met hers. 'You are so talented. Why haven't you pursued this as a career? You have a gift. I'm not just saying it, you truly do. I have never seen such mastery of perspective and use of light and colour.'

Jade was stunned by his reaction. She had tried to be objective with her work but she always felt as if she could do better, that she was not good enough and never would be. She had no background in the arts; she hadn't studied art history or worked with an established artist in a mentor programme, as so many others did. She hadn't read a single textbook on technique or style because she couldn't. She had looked at the pictures, certainly, but that didn't really count for much, in her opinion. She had acted out so much during her childhood, from frustration at not being able to understand what the teachers were trying to teach her, that her behaviour had been what everyone had focused on, each school she had attended failing to recognise that her disruptive behaviour was a symptom rather than the cause. As the years went on she had felt too ashamed to tell anyone of her inability to read past a few simple words. Her dependency on her father had never been a choice, for how could she expect anyone to employ her with no literacy skills?

Nic put the paintings to one side and placed his hands on shoulders. 'Why are you hiding your talent away?' he asked. 'Why let everyone believe you are nothing but a time-wasting society heiress when you have this incredible gift?'

Jade twisted her mouth. 'It's nice of you to be

so positive but I'm not exactly a gifted artist. I know nothing about art theory. I just do what I feel like at the time. Sometimes it works, sometimes it doesn't. Mostly, it doesn't.'

'*Cara*, you are being so hard on yourself,' he said. 'I just don't understand. You, of all people. You've had the money to back you to go to the art school of your choice. You have the sort of networking opportunities most struggling artists would kill for and yet you have hidden all of this away as if it's some dreadful, shameful secret. Why?'

Jade moved out from under his gently cupping hands and folded her arms across her middle, her face turned away to look out of the window to the bubbling fountain way below. 'I prefer it this way,' she said. 'When you have spent all of your life in the public's eye as I have done, it is nice to know there is at least one area you can keep private. This is mine.'

Nic frowned as he studied her. She had that keep-your-distance aura about her again, which he hadn't seen in days. He had thought he was finally breaking down some of the barriers she kept putting up. He had enjoyed seeing her relax her guard around him. He had enjoyed seeing her smile and once, when she'd laughed at something he had said, he'd felt a warm feeling spreading like hot honey deep inside his chest. It seemed as if each day he discovered something new about her. Like how her skin tasted when she had been in the sun: hot and silky and delicious. How her green eyes darkened when she looked at him when he was about to kiss her, and the way her hands felt sliding over him, over his back or chest, or the way she cupped him and stroked him until he felt as if the control he had always prided himself on was like a wisp of smoke, about to slip out of his grasp.

He was discovering things about himself too. How much he liked the way her dark, silky hair tickled his chest when she lay across him after making love, when in the past he had always preferred blondes. He liked the way her body felt as it gripped him so tightly, as if he was her first and only lover. In a way he felt as if he was. He dismissed those who had gone before as exploitative creeps who had lusted after her for all the wrong reasons. Nic liked how she continued to surprise him. He had grown increasingly bored with the women he had dated recently. They looked good and they had felt good, but he had not had an in-depth conversation with any one of them.

Jade had layers to her character that he was only starting to peel away—interesting, captivating layers that hinted at a deeply sensitive, gifted and intelligent young woman who, for some strange reason, was doing her best to keep that side of herself hidden as if she was somehow ashamed of it.

He was determined to get to know everything there was to know about his wife.

His wife.

He almost laughed out loud. His grandfather had pulled a swift one on him, that was for sure, making certain he was well and truly shackled in matrimony. But more than a week had gone by already and Nic was starting to think about how it would feel closer to the time to end it. He hadn't thought too much about that part of things before; he had simply concentrated on securing his inheritance. That had been his main priority and Jade's too, when it came to that. She had made it clear she wanted the money and, unless she decided to enter the workforce or sell some of her paintings, she was going to need every penny of it to live the life she had said she wanted to live.

Would he get so used to having her in his life that getting her out of it would prove a little too difficult?

He suppressed another laugh. Of course not! He wasn't the falling in love type. He had always lived in the fast lane. Settling down to domesticity, even with his wealth, which made his life easier than most, was out of the question. He was a freedom lover. He liked the ability to come and go as he pleased. He didn't want to answer to anyone but himself. He couldn't envisage himself any other way.

But looking at her with that faraway look on

her face made him ache with need for her. How did she do it to him? It was like a magnetic force that kept luring him towards her. He had made love to her only that morning and yet his body was hardening as he thought of taking her now.

She turned from the window and saw him looking at her. Her eyes darkened and his blood began to pound. She sent the point of her tongue—the tongue that only this morning had tasted him intimately—across her lips and gave him the look—the look that he could not, in this lifetime at least, seem to resist.

'Come here,' he commanded.

She gave a little haughty lift of her chin but he saw through it for the game it was. 'Why don't *you* come here?' she said.

'I want you over here.'

She slowly walked towards him, tempting him every step of the way with her coquettish smile and gently swaying slim hips. 'And you always get what you want, don't you, Italian boy?' she said in a husky whisper as she placed both of her hands flat on his chest.

Nic smiled as her hands slid down, all the way down over his abdomen to brush against his erection. 'So far,' he said and sealed her mouth with his.

She kissed him with her whole body, wrapping her arms around his neck, her fingers lacing through his hair until he felt a shiver of anticipation course down his spine. She pushed herself against him, her pelvis exciting him as it rubbed against his. His tongue played with hers, stroking and cajoling and then stabbing and thrusting as his need for her escalated. He loved her in this mood, so playful and teasing, making him want her as much as she wanted him.

Loved her?

His mind slammed on the brakes. This wasn't about love. It was about lust. He wanted her body and that was all he wanted. And she was offering it to him in the most delightful way possible.

He cupped her breasts and heard her whimper in response. He peeled her loose-fitting top off her shoulder and kissed his way down her neck, moving aside her bra to take her nipple in his mouth. She dug her fingers into his hair and arched her spine like a cat, inciting him further. She tasted so fresh and feminine and irresistible. He wanted her so badly he felt his body straining against his clothes. But, as if she sensed his discomfort, she started to deal with it by unhooking his belt and sliding down his zip, her dancing fingers wreaking havoc on his senses.

Nic fought for control as she caressed him, slowly at first, up and down his shaft, taking her time, making each pleasurable sensation ramp up his desire. His abdomen clenched like a fist as she went to her knees in front of him, her moistened lips moving closer and closer…

'You don't have to do that,' he croaked. 'I don't expect it of you.'

She looked up at him with sultry green eyes. 'I want to do it,' she said in that same husky tone she had used earlier.

Nic swallowed as she moved closer, her pink tongue coming out to lick him like a kitten did at its first taste of milk. He felt every nerve twitch and fire, lightning-fast blood filling him to bursting point as she did it again, slower this time, long slow strokes that sent him into a tailspin of want. He couldn't speak, he couldn't even think beyond what he was feeling right at this point. Her tongue continued its sensual teasing and then she opened her mouth over him, taking him in bit by bit, sucking, pulling, withdrawing and then doing it all over again. He tried to anchor himself by holding her head with his hands, but she took that as encouragement and went harder and faster. He knew then he had no possible hope of stopping this runaway train. He came with a burst of cannon fire that sent colours exploding like fireworks in his head. He shuddered his way through it, almost folding at the knees as she milked him for every last drop of his essence.

And that was another thing that totally surprised him. It didn't feel like it had in the past. This time it felt sacred, as if something elemental had just occurred between them, something that was not so easily reversed.

Nic didn't want to think too deeply about

exactly what it was. Instead, he brought her to her feet and slid his hands down her body, cupping her feminine mound, which was delightfully humid and moist with her need of him. He laid her down on the floor, removing her clothes until she was totally naked. He drank in the sight of her, the way her breasts rounded out now she was flat on her back, the way her long, slim legs had opened for him, the secret heart of her swollen and ready for his possession.

He wasn't far off it either. He was already growing hard again and couldn't wait to feel her ripples of pleasure around him. 'I can never seem to get enough of you,' he said, kissing his way down her sternum. 'I want you even straight after I have just had you.'

'I want you too,' Jade said and gasped as he slid a finger inside her.

'You're so wet for me,' he said. 'I want you to be wet for me all the time.'

Jade felt utterly shameless as he caressed her to the brink of release. She whimpered and panted as he brought her close before backing off, as

if he wanted to prolong her pleasure for as long
as he could. She couldn't take it any more. She
wanted the precious release his body could give
and begged for it without demur. 'Make me
come,' she said. 'Please, Nic, make me come
now.'

He removed the rest of his clothes and posi-
tioned himself over her body, flinging one leg
over one of hers before he thrust into her, stron-
ger than he had ever done before. Pleasure shot
through her as he filled her to the hilt, her body
wrapping around him, squeezing him, delighting
in the power and potency of him as he worked
them both to a tumultuous orgasm.

Jade felt every wave of pleasure in every part
of her body. The aftershocks were just as pleasurable, leaving her relaxed and boneless in his
arms.

'You know something?' Nic said as he propped
himself up to look down at her.

She smiled coyly. 'What?'

He trailed a finger down the curve of her cheek,
setting her skin alight all over again. 'If we make

love in every room in this villa and my one back in Rome, the first year of our marriage will go so quickly it will be over before you know it.'

The year or our marriage or both? Jade wanted to ask but daren't. 'How many rooms are there here?' she asked instead, trying to ignore the fault line ache in her heart.

'Fifty or so, I think,' he said, sending his finger over her top lip, back and forth until it buzzed with sensation.

'And the one in Rome?' she asked, quivering as he began to nibble at her earlobe.

'Thirty or so,' he said. 'I have the perfect room in mind for your studio.'

She looked at him in surprise. 'You mean I can have another one?'

He smiled a glinting smile. 'You can have whatever you want.'

No, I can't, Jade thought sadly. *The thing I most want is way out of reach and always has been.* Nic wanted her for now. It was convenient for him, as convenient as their marriage. He didn't want her for ever.

His lips brushed hers softly. 'We should go out to dinner tonight. The press will expect us to surface by now. How about it? Do you fancy a night out?'

Jade would have much preferred a night in but sensed Nic was getting restless. He thrived on being around people and, after a week at the villa with only the skeleton staff around, he was probably going crazy for more stimulation.

'Sure,' she said with a forced smile. 'Why not?'

He gave her another quick kiss before he leapt to his feet, holding out a hand to her to help her up. 'You have the first shower while I sort out some business,' he said. 'I'll call and make a booking. Wear something sexy for me so I can fantasize about what I am going to do to you when we get home.'

Jade showered and then dressed the part of glamorous society wife, taking extra time over her hair and make-up. The designer dress she wore was black but cut in a classic style that highlighted her figure. She arranged her hair at the back of her head in a smooth, shiny chignon and, after spraying herself with her favourite perfume, she was about to put on a pair of earrings when Nic came behind her and handed her a flat, rectangular jewellery box.

'How about you wear these?' he said.

She took the box from him and carefully opened it. Inside were an exquisite diamond pendant and a pair of droplet earrings, the sheer brilliance of them taking her breath away. She had worn plenty of expensive jewellery in the past but nothing of this phenomenal quality. It was as if three bright stars had been plucked from the night sky and laid on the black velvet just for her pleasure. 'I don't know what to say…' She looked up at him. 'Are these for me to keep or did you hire them?'

He rolled his eyes at her. 'You think I am that cheap, *cara mio*?' he asked. 'Of course I didn't hire them. I bought them for you.'

'But it's not my birthday for days and days,' she said, looking back at the glittering diamonds.

'Does it have to be a special occasion for you to be given a gift?' he asked, tipping up her chin so her eyes meshed with his.

Jade felt the magnetic pull of his gaze. All her senses began to twitch with excitement at the way he was looking at her. Her need of him made her feel more and more vulnerable. She supposed that was why she said what she did before she stopped to think about it. 'Do you buy all your lovers expensive gifts?'

His mouth tensed at the edges. 'You are my wife, Jade. It is only right that I buy you things.'

'I'm not really your wife, not in the normal way,' she said. 'Or at least not for very long.'

'Then all the more reason to get what you can out of this marriage while you can,' he said. 'Money, jewellery and memories of the best sex you've ever have. Not such a bad deal, *sì*?'

Jade wanted to call him out on that but how could she? What he said was true. She was going to take all of that and more from this marriage when it ended. But instead she smiled coolly and elegantly rose to her feet.

'Will you help me put these on?' she asked, turning her back to him.

His hands made her neck fizz with sensation as he attached the pendant, and her heart began to race as she thought of him removing it later that evening, most probably along with the rest of her clothes.

'You smell divine,' he said in a low, husky voice next to her ear. 'If we had more time I would feast on you right here and now.'

She tilted her head to one side and closed her eyes, her breath coming out as a ragged stream as he trailed a fiery pathway of kisses down to her bare shoulder. His tongue rasped along her sensitive flesh, making her shiver all over.

'Do you need help with the earrings?' he asked against her collarbone.

'I'll be fine,' she said in a scratchy voice. 'Don't… you…um…need to shower and change?'

He stepped back from her. 'I won't be long. Wait for me downstairs, otherwise I might change my mind and drag you into the shower with me.'

Jade left the bedroom as soon as she put the earrings on because she didn't trust herself with him only metres away, naked and wet and all too irresistibly male.

CHAPTER NINE

NIC had booked them a table at the Terrazza Serbelloni at the Grand Hotel Villa Serbelloni, one of the most luxurious hotels fringing the shores of Lake Como. The restaurant overlooked the lake and, as the evening was warm and still, the water was as smooth as a sheet of glass.

They were led to their table and, once they had drinks ordered, Jade tried her best to relax. There had been no sign of the press and, while the staff had addressed Nic by name, they had retreated to the background, leaving her and Nic to contemplate the menu in peace.

She looked at the menu and chewed her lip in concentration. As usual, the words meant nothing to her. 'What are you thinking of having?' she asked after a moment.

'I think the fillet of turbot sounds good, but

then again the loin of lamb is tempting,' Nic said. 'What about you?'

Jade closed the menu. 'I'll have the fish.'

He cocked his head at her. 'You're very decisive. Don't you want a bit more time? There are lots of other things to choose from. This is an award-winning restaurant.'

'No, I'm good,' she said. 'I fancy fish. It's good for the brain, or so they say.'

Nic closed the menu after a few minutes and the waiter came over and took their orders.

Once he had left, Jade asked, 'You haven't thought of developing a rival hotel here?'

'I have thought about it but Giorgio would have my guts for garters if I went ahead with it,' he said. 'It will stay in the family until all three of us come to some agreement over what should be done with it. I think Luca and Bronte will use it a fair bit. It's a great place to get away from the press.'

'I can't believe it has been empty for so long,' she said musingly. 'It's such a beautiful place. I could sit for hours just looking out at the gardens.

It must take an awful lot of maintenance, even if it's not occupied very often.'

He gave her a rueful look over the top of his wine glass. 'It does and that is why I insisted on using it more. I am glad you like it. Hopefully, during this year we will get up here a few more times.'

Jade took a sip of her mineral water and then put her glass back down with careful precision to disguise the slight tremble of her hand. 'Do you think your family will be upset when we eventually divorce?' she asked.

He frowned as if he found the question annoying. 'It has nothing to do with them. It's about what we want.'

Jade already knew what he wanted; the trouble was, it wasn't the same as what she did. 'At the wedding, your mother seemed rather keen on the idea of us making a go of it,' she said. 'I didn't like to disillusion her. She thinks we will fall in love like your father eventually did with her.'

'My mother is a hopeless romantic,' he said, still frowning in irritation. 'She thinks no man is complete unless he is married with a family. When the time comes, she will have to accept the termination of our marriage just like everybody else.'

Including me, Jade thought sadly.

He looked at her with a serious expression carved into his features. 'It has to be this way, Jade. At the risk of repeating myself, you have to realise this isn't going to last.'

'How long has your longest relationship lasted?' she asked.

His frown tightened even further. 'What has that got to do with anything?'

Jade held his gaze with an effort. 'What if you still want me once the year is up?'

He shifted his mouth from side to side as he thought about it. 'We can continue our affair for as long as we like, but marriage in the long term is not an option for me. It's not that I have anything against marriage. I can see my brothers are both very happy, but it's not something I want for myself.'

Jade continued on the devil's advocate route.

'What about if you get tired of me before the year is up?'

'I can't see that happening,' he said with a glinting smile. 'You excite me, *cara*, like no other woman has done before.'

Jade felt a ripple of excitement move through her body. His eyes darkened with desire as they held hers, promising earth-shattering passion. 'Have you ever been in love?' she asked.

'No, have you?'

She looked down at her glass rather than hold his penetrating gaze. 'I thought I was once but now I realise it was just a crush. Real love, the lasting sort, I suspect, is something else entirely.'

'So you believe in lasting love?' he asked as he picked up his wine glass again.

Jade made herself meet his eyes. 'I think it can happen, sure. I think there is probably a bit of luck involved, you know, meeting at the right time, having similar goals and values. I am sure it's hard work at times, all relationships are, but if both parties are committed and willing to go the distance, I can see it could be a very satisfying thing.'

'So once the ink is dry on our divorce papers, are you going to immediately set out to hunt down a husband and father for your children?' he asked.

Jade sent him a frowning look. 'I told you: I don't want children.'

He smiled cynically. 'So you say now at not quite twenty-six, but what will you say in five or ten years?'

'I could ask you the same question,' she quickly threw back.

'Ah, yes, but I do not have a biological clock to worry about,' he pointed out. 'I can father a child, should I choose to do so, at almost any age.'

Jade didn't like being reminded of the clock ticking inside her. She sometimes heard it late at night when she couldn't sleep. She worried about missing out on such a wondrous experience as giving birth to her very own child, but what sort of mother would *she* make? She would be as hopeless at it as she was at so many other things.

It wouldn't be fair on the child to have such an inadequately prepared mother. The child would end up embarrassed and ashamed of her even before it was of school age. There were some things you could hide from adults, but children were incredibly perceptive. She had already had a couple of close calls with Julianne McCormack's children, who had picked up on her reluctance to perform certain tasks they took for granted in their mother doing for them, like reading a bedtime story.

'You have gone very quiet, Jade,' Nic said. 'What are you frowning about? Have I touched on a sensitive nerve?'

'Not at all,' she said, raising her chin. 'I guess not all women are cut out to be mothers.'

He tapped his fingers on the rim of his glass as he continued to study her. 'Has your reluctance to reproduce got something to do with your dysfunctional family?'

Jade bristled defensively. 'No, why should it? Lots of people come from broken or dysfunctional homes and they still go on to have children of their own.'

'You lost your mother so young,' he said. 'Don't you think that might be why you are so against having children in case the same happens to them? Perhaps you are worried they might go through the trauma and loss you did.'

'Why are we even having this conversation?' she asked, trying not to show how seriously rattled she was. 'It's pointless. Neither of us wants children. I don't see why I have to be cross-examined like this.'

'I am not trying to upset you, *cara*, I am simply trying to understand you,' he said. 'You are like a difficult puzzle. There are pieces you seem to be deliberately hiding from me.'

She glowered at him resentfully. 'As far as I see it, you know far more about me than anyone. But I don't see the use in becoming bosom buddies as well as sex buddies.'

The corner of his mouth lifted. 'Is that how you see us, just as sex buddies?'

'It's true, isn't it?' she said. 'We scratch each other's itch.'

'It's one hell of an itch,' he said with another glinting smile.

Jade dabbed at her mouth with her napkin. 'Would you excuse me?' she asked, pushing back her chair. 'I need to use the bathroom.'

'But of course,' he said, rising politely as she left the table.

Jade let out a breath of air when she got to the ladies' room. Her face was flushed with colour and her skin felt tight all over. She took a few minutes to gather herself. Nic was pushing on buttons she didn't want pushed. She didn't understand his motives. He was adamant their relationship was finite. Why then badger her with questions that were so deeply personal? It was unsettling to have to face such interrogation. She was so frightened she would betray herself by confessing her love for him. Making love with him made it almost impossible not to whisper the words. She had come so close so many times.

He made her flesh sing and her heart ache with the weight of the love she felt for him, but telling him would make things so much worse for her. It would drive him into another woman's arms for sure.

Jade came out of the ladies' room and was half-way back to the table when a hand came down on her arm. She stopped in her tracks and looked at the man who had stalled her. Her heart gave a sickening thud in her chest and her mouth went completely dry.

'Jade,' Tim Renshaw-Heath said with a sleazy smile. 'Long time no see. What, it must be over a year now, right? How are you? Are you here with someone?'

'Yes,' she said, pulling her arm away. 'I am here with my husband.'

Tim's blond brows rose. 'Married, huh? Somehow I didn't see you as the settling-down type.'

Jade flicked her gaze to their table, but Nic was scrolling through his text messages on his phone. She tried to move away but Tim blocked her with his short but stocky frame. 'Hey, don't rush off,' he said and reached into his jacket pocket and held out a business card. 'Call me if you get sick of your husband or if he's out of town some time. I can fill in for him if you know what I mean. I'm still at the same apartment in London. Maybe this time you won't stand me up, eh?'

Jade felt sick to her stomach at his crude suggestion. She ignored the business card and gave him an icy look. 'I am not interested in betraying my marriage vows.'

His porcine eyes gleamed. 'I think I could get you to change your mind.' He fanned open his wallet in front of her face. 'Perhaps this is what I should have offered you the first time around, eh? How much, Jade? How much to sample that delectable body of yours?'

Jade hadn't heard Nic approach but she saw Tim take a step backwards as he hurriedly stuffed his wallet back into his pocket.

'If you ever insult my wife again, I will personally see to it that you never step into this or any other five-star hotel in any country in Europe,'

Nic said through clenched teeth. 'Do you understand or do I need to press home my point some other, shall we say, more physical way?'

Jade put her hand on Nic's tensely muscled arm. 'Nic, no, please, it's not worth it. He's not worth it.'

'Ah, but *you* are, *cara mio*,' Nic said before turning to glare at the other man with eyes as cold and hard as green and brown flecked marbles.

Tim moved away, or slunk away was probably a more accurate description. He seemed to shrink even further in height as Nic's tall figure towered over him in an intimidating manner.

'We're leaving,' Nic said, taking her by the hand with firm fingers.

Jade didn't bother arguing. She couldn't wait to get away from the curious glances they had attracted. She felt thoroughly ashamed of her past and wished she could make it all go away. How had she been so lacking in self-esteem and self-worth to flirt with someone as boorish as Tim Renshaw-Heath? It disgusted her that she had such skeletons in her closet. It didn't matter that she hadn't slept with him or even half of the men the press had made out. The way Tim and his ilk treated her made her feel as if she had, and that, for some reason, was far worse.

Nic didn't speak until they were back at the villa. Jade glanced at him a couple of times but his mouth was set in a flat line and his eyes were still flashing with fury, his fists clenching and un-clenching as if he was mentally landing a punch on the other man's face.

The door closed with a resounding echo as he slammed it once they were home. 'You should not have spoken to him,' he said through tight lips. 'You should have ignored him as if you didn't know who the hell he was and come straight back to me.'

Jade swallowed to clear her blocked throat. 'I'm sorry—I didn't see him until he put his hand on my arm. I didn't want to cause a scene in the middle of the restaurant.'

He glared at her. 'Damn it, Jade, is this how it's going to be for the next year?'

She felt her back come up. 'Aren't you being a little hypocritical here, Nic? After all, you've had numerous lovers. It's just as likely we will run into one or two or more of them while we are married, especially as you insist on me travelling with you.'

His eyes hardened as they tethered hers. 'It's not the same thing at all. My relationships had some context, some meaning, even if they were not long term.'

Jade straightened her spine. 'Just what exactly are you saying?'

His expression was dark and brooding with tension. 'I think you know what I am saying.'

'Actually, I don't,' she said, defiantly meeting his gaze. 'Why don't you spell it out for me?'

He raked a hand through his hair, his throat moving up and down over a lumpy swallow. 'I don't like the thought of you being spoken to by men like that sleaze ball back there,' he said. 'I don't like the thought of men like him treating you as if you're some sort of high street whore. You're not and you never have been.'

Jade felt tears bank up in her eyes. He was showing a depth of protection and care she could not have hoped anyone would have shown towards her, let alone him.

Nic's frown cut into his forehead. 'Why are you crying, *cara*?'

Jade brushed at her eyes. 'B…because you don't think I'm a slut…' Her voice tripped over a little sob.

He came over and enveloped her in his arms, resting his head on the top of hers. '*Mio piccolo*,' he said softly. 'Of course I don't think you are any such thing.'

She looked up at him but kept her arms wrapped around his waist. 'It's not like you think, Nic,' she said. 'I didn't sleep with Tim or even half of the men the press have reported I've been with. I let everyone think I was a tart but deep down I hate that label. I wish I could make it go away.'

He took out his handkerchief and gently blotted the tears coursing down her cheeks. 'I have things in my past I would like to forget about too—everyone does, I would imagine. The thing is to show the world you don't care. If you ever meet someone from your past, ignore them, move on without engaging in idle chit-chat. They will want to drag you down to their level but they can only do that if you let them. Hold your head high, *tesore mio*. You deserve respect. You're beautiful and talented and have a caring, gentle nature when you're not too busy pushing everyone away.'

Jade placed one of her hands on the side of his face, stroking his cleanly shaven jaw. 'I wish there were more men like you in the world, men of quality and decency.'

He gave her a rueful smile. 'You wouldn't be calling me decent if you knew what I was thinking right now.'

She smiled coyly up at him. 'What are you thinking?'

He brought her close to his growing erection, his hands warm and strong as they cupped her bottom. 'How is that for a clue?' he asked with a dangerously sexy look.

'I think I'm more or less getting the message,'

she said, moving against him, delighting in the way his eyes darkened in response.

His mouth came down to meet hers in a kiss that was blisteringly hot. Jade's lips felt like fire as he plundered her mouth, his tongue sweeping against hers, calling it into a sexy duel that made all her senses sing with delight. Her whole body erupted into flames of longing, her inner core pulsing with the need to feel his hard presence moving inside her.

He scooped her effortlessly into his arms and carried her upstairs to the master suite. He laid her on the bed and then stood and stripped off his clothes, his eyes never once straying from hers.

Jade could feel her excitement building. Her blood began to speed through her veins as her eyes went to his aroused length. She licked her lips and scrambled onto her knees on the mattress, wriggling out of her dress and lacy bra and knickers and tossing them over the side of the bed. She went to undo the pendant from around her neck but Nic's hand came out and stopped her.

'No, let me make love to you wearing nothing but diamonds,' he said and kissed the valley between her breasts where the pendant hung in sparkling brilliance.

There was something decidedly decadent and yet affirming about being pleasured whilst wearing priceless jewellery, Jade decided. She felt like a princess, a person of worth instead of the trashy home-wrecking whore she had been portrayed as in the past.

Nic's mouth closed over one of her breasts, his tongue teasing her nipple until she was arching her spine in rapture. He worked his way from her nipples to the sensitive undersides of her breasts, stroking and gently nipping with his teeth, making every atom of her being crave his final possession.

He went from her breasts over the flat plane of her belly, his tongue circling then diving into the little bowl of her belly button. Her nerves twitched and danced under the ministrations of his lips and tongue, her mind becoming vacant of everything apart from how he made her feel.

He moved lower, taking his time as he separated her tender folds. His tongue tasted her nectar, the intimate action sending sparks of electricity up and down her spine. Her toes curled, her belly flipped and flopped and her heart raced, her breathing becoming choppy as he intensified his caresses, his jungle cat-like licks making her edge closer and closer to the release she wanted so badly. Her fingers dug into his thick hair in an attempt to hold herself steady in a sea of sensation that was pitching and rocking her about like a bit of flotsam.

She cried out when the first ripples of her orgasm rolled through her, the sheer force of it as it gathered momentum making her mind go blank.

He moved back up her body, his need for her so obvious she couldn't help but reach out to stroke him, to feel the pulse of his blood as it extended him so powerfully. He groaned as she moved her hand harder and faster, and then, with another muttered imprecation, he sought her moist warmth, driving into her with a slick thrust that sent a shower of fireworks off in her brain.

He set a fast pace but she quickly caught his rhythm, moving her pelvis in time with his, accepting each of his hard thrusts with a clutch of her inner muscles until he shouted out loud as he came. She felt the pumping action of his body, the hot spill of his life force anointing her as she lay there quivering in reaction.

His face was buried against her neck, his breathing hot and hectic against her skin. 'Am I too heavy for you?' he asked.

'No,' she said, smiling to herself as his big, strong body pinned her to the bed. She loved the weight of him; it made her feel sensuous to have her limbs entwined so intimately with his and to have his maleness encased in the secret feminine vault of her body.

He came up on his elbows and pressed a soft kiss to her mouth. 'You are beautiful, do you know that?' he said.

Jade wasn't vain. She knew she had inherited from her mother high cheekbones, a neat, slightly uptilted nose, gloriously thick long hair and unusually green eyes, but she had never truly thought of herself as beautiful because she couldn't do the things she most wanted to do, the things most people took for granted. Perhaps beauty and brains didn't go together, after all, she thought. She had certainly missed out on the latter.

'Hey,' Nic said, taking her chin between his finger and thumb. 'What is that serious look for?'

Jade tried to smile but it didn't quite work. 'I was just thinking how I am going to miss this when it's over,' she said truthfully.

His brows moved together and his chest rose and fell as he let out a sigh. He rolled away and looked up at the ceiling, not speaking for a long minute. 'I know,' he finally said in a husky-sounding voice.

Jade waited for a few beats before she turned on her side to look at him. 'Will you miss me?' she said. 'I mean when we finally part company? I'll probably go back to live in London or maybe I'll go to Australia. I've always wanted to go. Have you been?'

He got off the bed and snatched up his trousers, his eyes moving away from hers. 'Yes, it's a great place to visit. I wish I'd had more time when I was there. You should go. The press wouldn't know who you were out there. You would have a chance at the fresh start you said you'd like to have.'

Jade couldn't read his expression. It was like a mask, and his voice had been curt, brusque and to the point, as if he didn't want to continue the conversation any longer than he had to. 'Nic?'

'What?' he asked, still frowning darkly as he faced her after shrugging himself back into his shirt.

She bit her lip, stung by the way he was shutting her out. 'Nothing,' she said.

'Look, Jade,' he said, scoring a rough pathway through his hair with his splayed fingers. 'You know the score. I have been totally honest with you about how far I am prepared to go. Don't go changing the rules, OK?'

She rolled her lips together and slowly lowered her gaze. 'I'm not changing the rules,' she said softly. 'I was merely saying I would miss what we've had when it's gone.'

'What do you want me to say, for God's sake?' he asked in a biting tone. 'That I will miss it too?'

She brought her gaze back to his. 'Will you?'

His eyes held hers for a throbbing second or two. 'I haven't given it a moment's thought,' he said and, without another word, he left the room, the door closing behind him like a punctuation mark on the conversation.

CHAPTER TEN

Nic announced over breakfast the following morning that they would be returning to Rome, a decision Jade assumed meant their honeymoon was effectively over. She suspected he was putting a wall up between them, a suspicion that was confirmed as soon as they returned to his villa close to the Villa Borghese.

Although he still joined her in bed at night and made love to her as passionately as ever, he didn't engage in lengthy conversations, or even trivial ones for that matter. When he wasn't putting in long hours at his office, he spent a lot of time in his study or on the phone, conducting his business matters with the sort of focus and drive she could only envy.

A new housekeeper was appointed without any input from Jade, but thankfully the woman Nic had chosen was friendly and helpful, even effusively admiring the sketches Jade brought in each day after her treks around the city.

Jade lost track of time as she wandered through the cobbled streets and alleyways as well as the major tourist drawcards. She spent hours at The Vatican, staring up at the ceiling of the Sistine Chapel until the guards urged her on. She made sketches of The Vatican and St Paul's Basilica and a sheltered glade in the Villa Borghese, as well as some street scenes that captured the essence of the Eternal City.

On Friday she spent the morning at the Colosseum, and then did another afternoon tour of The Vatican. And then, on a whim, she walked back to do some window shopping. She stopped outside a baby wear shop, looking at the tiny clothes with a tight ache in her heart. Her desire to be a mother seemed to increase more and more every day. It was such a no-go area with Nic. She couldn't understand why he was so adamant when he was clearly so fond of his little niece and nephews. Luca and Bronte had called in only a couple of evenings ago and again Jade had watched Nic play with Ella. He had swung her around in what Ella called a 'whizzy dizzy'. Nic had gone round and round with her in his arms until the little toddler was giggling uncontrollably. It had been such a happy family scene and Jade ached to be a part of it. Instead, she felt on the outside again, looking in, a spectator instead of a participant.

She went into the shop and picked up a little Babygro, a pink one with white polka dots. She ran her fingers over the velvet-soft fabric, wishing, hoping and dreaming for her life to be like Maya's and Bronte's. They were so deeply in love with their husbands and Giorgio and Luca were equally devoted.

Jade wasn't sure what made her look up at that point. A member of the press was standing outside the shop with his camera aimed straight at her. She put down the little suit and walked out, keeping her head down, ignoring the questions as they were fired at her.

'Are you expecting the next Sabbatini heir, *signora*?'

She moved past him and two other people who had stopped to stare.

'Is your husband pleased about the prospect of a son or daughter some time in the future?'

She skirted around another group of tourists and ducked down a side street but the journalist persisted.

'Is this a honeymoon baby?'

Jade finally managed to escape by slipping in amongst a guided tour group. Once the cameraman had gone, she walked back in the direction of Nic's villa. She was about halfway there when from inside her handbag she could hear her mobile ringing and quickly dug it out and pressed the answer button. 'Hello?'

'Jade, where are you?' Nic asked. 'I've just got home. It's after six. Why didn't you leave a note to tell me where you were?'

'I've been out sketching and then shopping,' she said, stepping out of the way of some tourists who were busily snapping their camera phones at the scenery.

'You could have at least sent me a text,' he said, sounding distinctly annoyed.

'I didn't want to bother you,' she said. 'You seem rather busy lately.'

'Feeling neglected, *cara*?'

'Not at all,' she responded tartly. 'I know you have things to do. So have I.'

'I haven't just been working on my own stuff. I have been working on setting up a meeting for you with an art gallery owner,' he said. 'He's coming at seven this evening to look at your work.'

Jade felt her skin break out in a sweat. 'Why? I told you it's mostly rubbish. I don't want anyone to see it, let alone a gallery owner. I can just imagine what he's going to say. I'll be mortified.'

'He will give an unbiased opinion,' Nic said. 'You have no need to get into a state about it. Constructive feedback is important, in any case.'

'I don't appreciate you interfering with my

private life,' she said as she walked briskly back the other way along the footpath, her agitation rising with every step.

'Jade, you are being childish about this. And of course I have the right to interfere in your private life. I am your husband.'

'Only for the next eleven months,' she said with cutting emphasis.

There was a silence that lasted only a couple of seconds but, even so, it seemed more than a little menacing.

'I will see you when you get back,' he said in a clipped tone. 'The art guy will be here in less than an hour. Don't be late.'

'Don't tell me what to do,' Jade shot back but he had already rung off.

When Jade got back to the villa after taking a lengthy detour, which included a coffee to fill in the time, Nic was fuming. He threw open the door as she came in, his eyes blazing with anger. 'Do you have any idea of what you might have just thrown away?' he asked. 'Clyde Prentham waited over an hour for you. He's an extremely busy man and he made a special effort to be here to meet you. He left just a few minutes ago.'

Jade tossed her head and stalked past but he captured her by the arm and turned her to face him. 'Let me go,' she said, glaring at him.

'Jade,' he said, this time lowering his voice. 'You seem to want to deliberately sabotage any chance at a career.'

She tugged on his hold but his fingers were like a manacle of steel. 'You don't understand,' she said, terrifyingly close to tears. 'I don't want to have my work analysed and judged and laughed at.'

Nic frowned and slowly loosened his grip to more of a caress on her arm. 'Why are you so worried about what people think of your art when you don't give a toss for what they think about you as a person? You seem to have it the wrong way about, *cara*. You let people say hideous things about you in the press without defending yourself and yet you hide your amazing talent as if it is something you are embarrassed about.'

Jade blinked back the blur of tears that were banking at the back of her eyes. 'I bet your art guy didn't say I was amazingly talented.' She brushed at her eyes with her free hand. 'I bet he thought you dragging him here was a complete and utter waste of time.'

'Actually, he was very impressed,' Nic said, stroking her wrist with his thumb.

She looked up at him with a guarded look. 'You're just saying that...'

He sent his eyes upwards in a frustrated roll. 'Why do you doubt yourself so much? Of course he was impressed. He said you have a very special way with colour and light. He couldn't believe you hadn't had tuition of any sort. You have natural talent, Jade. He wants to show some of your work, a limited space in a general exhibition to start with to get a feel for the market. He thinks you could have your own exhibition eventually.'

Jade thought of all that would entail. The business side of things would be her downfall. She would end up looking a fool, not even able to read through a contract or write her own biography for promotional purposes. She would be mocked in the press—the illiterate artist who could paint but not write down her own address.

'Why are you chewing at your lip like that?' Nic asked, brushing her savaged lip with his thumb.

'I can't do it, Nic,' she said. 'Please don't make me.'

'*Cara*, no one is making you do anything you don't want. If you don't feel ready to put your stuff out there, then that is your decision. It's just that I thought you would be interested in having something to fall back on should you need it in the future.'

She sent him a pointed look. 'Don't you mean when our marriage comes to an end and I've spent all the money? That's what you think, isn't it? That I'm going to spend all the money your grandfather left me and have nothing to show for it.'

His frown deepened across his forehead. 'I don't think that at all. I just don't believe you will be content with all that money unless you have a purpose for your life. Art is meant to be seen and appreciated. I don't understand why you won't take this chance to show the world you are not the shallow socialite everyone thinks you are.'

Jade turned away, not sure she could keep her emotions in check with his penetrating gaze focused on her. 'Let me think about it,' she said, knowing full well what her decision would be.

There was a small silence.

'You won't budge on this, will you?' he said.

She let out a tiny sigh and slowly turned around. 'My art is the one thing I can keep private,' she said. 'Like you and your brothers, I have lived my whole life in the public eye. This is one area I can keep to myself. It's an outlet for me. I do it because I love it, not because I have a deadline or a contract or an exhibition looming. I just love it.'

Nic gave her a crooked smile. 'You constantly surprise me, do you know that?'

Jade bit her lip again. 'I appreciate what you

were trying to do for me, Nic, I really do. I'm just not ready to take that step.'

He slowly nodded, as if he finally accepted her position. 'So, tell me about your shopping trip,' he said. 'Did you buy anything?'

Jade felt her colour blast like an open furnace on her cheeks. 'Um…no…I didn't.'

'Any paparazzi lurking around?'

She had to look away, her gaze going to the gardens outside. 'They're pretty hard to avoid,' she said. 'You know how it is.'

'Yes, I do indeed,' he said, coming up behind her to place his hands on her shoulders.

Jade felt her whole body shiver in reaction. She automatically leant backwards, seeking his hard warmth. He brought his mouth down to the sensitive skin of her neck, just beneath the thick curtain of her hair, his teeth nibbling at her playfully, sending every nerve into a madcap frenzy.

'You always taste so delicious,' he murmured against her neck. 'I can't keep my hands or my mouth off you.'

'Maybe after eleven months you won't feel quite

the same way,' Jade said, desperately looking for reassurance.

Nic turned her around in one movement, his eyes dark and frowning. 'Why do you have to keep on about that?' he asked. 'You know the terms. We stay in this marriage until we get what we both want. That's the deal. You signed on it, Jade. You read the contract. It's in black and white with your signature at the bottom of it.'

Jade moved out of his hold, cupping her elbows with her palms. 'Don't you ever think about anything else but money?' she asked. 'You drive yourself so hard in business, but what for? Who are you going to give it to when you leave this earth?'

He looked at her for a tense moment before turning away to rub at a knot of tension at the back of his neck. 'I haven't any plans to leave this earth for the next sixty-odd years if I am lucky.'

'You can't know what life will have in store for you,' she said. 'No one can.'

'I realise that, Jade, but you have to be sensible

about this. This was never about the long term. We both agreed on that. When this is over, I want my life to continue the way it always has.'

'But what if it can't?' she asked. 'What if this year changes everything?'

He frowned at her. 'What do you mean?'

'What if that's what your grandfather wanted to communicate to you by tying things up the way he did?' she asked. 'You can't have life the way you want it, Nic. It doesn't work out that way. Sometimes things happen that change everything and you can't change it back.'

He cocked his head at a wary angle. 'What sort of things are we talking about here?'

She bit her lip and looked away. 'Nothing specific.'

'Jade?' He turned her with one hand, forcing her chin up to meet his gaze. 'What is going on?'

Her green eyes flickered with something but then she lowered her gaze. 'I'm just tired,' she said.

Nic brushed his thumb across her cheek. 'I

can see that. You look pale and you have dark smudges under your eyes. Why don't you go to bed and I'll sleep in one of the spare rooms tonight?'

She looked at him with a nervous flicker of her gaze. 'You don't have to do that...'

He pressed a soft kiss to the little frown in between her finely arched brows. 'Oh, but I do, *cara mio*,' he said softly. 'Otherwise I will keep you up all hours pleasuring you because I can't stop myself.'

She gave him a small movement of her lips that wasn't quite a smile. 'Well, goodnight, then,' she said and stepped away.

Nic caught her hand on the way past, closing his fingers around hers for a fleeting moment. He felt the tingles all the way up his arm, the flow of his blood increasing its pace as her fingers moved against his. But then her hand slipped out of his and she was gone, her soft footsteps fading into the distance.

He stood staring at the space where she had been for a long moment, a frown pulling at his forehead as he pictured their final goodbye in eleven months' time. His stomach felt wrapped in barbed wire as he imagined that parting scene: the final handover of money, the polite goodbyes and 'thanks for the memories' routine. Why had his grandfather locked them together like this when it would only cause grief and pain when it ended?

It doesn't have to end...

Nic shook his head as if to get rid of the errant thought. Of course it had to end. Jade had the right to her own life—a life with someone who could give her the things she wanted. She believed in lasting love and she deserved it. No one deserved it more. She said she didn't want children but he wasn't sure if she was being truthful on that. He had seen her with his nephews and niece, the way her face lit up and her smile bloomed like an exotic and rare flower.

He thought about her vulnerability. She pretended to be so tough but inside she was like a frightened little girl. Who would be around to protect her if he wasn't? If they divorced as planned she would be even more vulnerable. She would be such an easy target for some creep after her money. She had a naivety about her that, in spite of her street-smart past, had never really gone away.

Letting her go was not going to be easy. He had not expected their time together to be so intensely satisfying. He ached for her and couldn't imagine how this need he felt so constantly was going to ever fade.

Maybe it wouldn't...

He frowned until his forehead hurt. It had to fade. It always did. He had never fallen in love. Love was not an emotion he trusted. Sure, he loved his family and would put his life on the line for any one of them, but romantic love was something that came and went. It was unreliable and transient. He had no intention of allowing himself to be sucked into the fantasy of happily ever after, although he had to admit that in some cases, such as his brothers' lives, it actually was a reality and not a fantasy at all.

He gave a cynical laugh but it caught on something deep in his chest.

Maybe there was hope for him after all.

CHAPTER ELEVEN

WHEN Jade woke up the next morning Nic was standing by the bedside with a newspaper in his hand. 'What is the meaning of this?' he asked, thrusting it at her.

Jade frowned as she pushed her tousled hair out of her eyes. She glanced at the paper before returning her eyes to his glittering ones. 'You know I can't read Italian,' she said. 'Why don't you read it to me?'

'Here's an English paper,' he said, pushing another paper towards her. 'It says much the same thing.'

She looked at a photograph of her in the baby wear shop the day before. She couldn't read the caption but the photo told the story: she was holding the pink with polka dots Babygro, looking down at it with a dreamy, wistful look on her face.

'Well?'

Jade looked at him. 'It's not what you think.'

'Then why don't you tell me what it is?' His voice contained a thread of steel.

She decided to be honest with him. 'Nic, I can't go on like this. I have to be honest with you.'

'Is this another one of your attention-seeking tricks?' He stabbed a finger at the paper. 'To tell the press you were pregnant before you even told me?'

Jade looked at him in shock. *'Is that what it says?'*

His frown deepened. 'What, you're not pregnant?'

'No, of course not,' she said. 'How could you think that? I told you I was on the Pill. I wouldn't deliberately try and trap you like that.'

Nic dropped the paper and rubbed a hand over his unshaven face. 'I'm sorry, Jade,' he said. 'Just like everyone else, I immediately jumped to the wrong conclusion.'

'It's OK.'

'No, it's not OK,' he said. 'I'm the one who

should know better. I know you. I should not have judged you so quickly.'

'You don't really know me, Nic,' Jade said softly. 'You don't know me at all.'

'How can you say that?' he asked. 'Of course I know you.'

'Do you know what I want most in the world?' she asked.

His expression faltered for a moment. 'You want to be loved,' he said. 'I know that you want to be loved and accepted for who you are.'

'Do you love and accept me as I am?'

His throat moved up and down over a rough swallow. 'I care about you, Jade,' he said in a gruff tone. 'I admit I didn't at first. I was annoyed that we were forced to marry. I couldn't think of anyone I wanted to marry less. But I have come to see how wrong I was about you. You are a very special person. So talented, so beautiful and so damned sensual I can't keep my hands off you.'

He cares for me, Jade thought with a mental curl of her lip. What a pathetic word that was.

People cared for their goldfish and pot plants, for God's sake. It didn't mean they would give anything to be with them. It didn't mean they felt achingly empty when they were away from them. It didn't mean they couldn't imagine life without them in it. She felt all that and more for Nic. Surely she deserved to be loved, not just cared about.

'*Cara?*' He stroked a gentle thumb across her cheek. 'We're good together. You know we are. We care about each other. That is a good thing, *sì?*'

'How do you know what I feel about you?' Jade asked. 'I might still hate you for all you know.'

His thumb moved to stroke across her bottom lip. 'If you do, you have a delightful way of showing it.'

Jade pulled away from his tempting touch. 'Nic, I want some space…to think about things.'

He frowned darkly. 'Things? What things?'

She chewed at her lip where his thumb had set off the nerves into a tingling frenzy. 'The news thing…the false report about a pregnancy? Well,

I've kind of changed my mind about babies and… things…'

Nic's frown intensified until his brows met over his eyes. 'Are you saying you *want* to have a baby?' he asked.

Jade held her breath for a moment before she answered. 'I know this is not what you want. And I know it's not really fair to spring it on you, so that's why I want some time to think about what happens after this year is over. I need time, Nic. Please, just let me go back to London for a few days. I can't think straight when I'm with you.'

'*Cara*, I can't think straight when I'm with you either but do you really have to go to London?' he asked. 'It'll be wet and cold, for one thing.'

Jade steeled her resolve. 'Just a few days, OK? Just until my birthday. I want to see Julianne McCormack. I want her to know I didn't betray our friendship. I need to do that face to face. I should have done that right at the start. At least now she knows we are married maybe she'll listen to me.'

He scraped a hand through his hair. 'I'll book

you a room in our London hotel. But I want to join you in a couple of days, got that? I am not having you out of my sight any longer than that.'

'Because you don't trust me?' Jade asked.

He gave her a long and serious look before he brushed the back of his knuckles down the curve of her cheek. 'Because I will miss you, *mio piccolo*,' he said.

London was as cold and wet as Nic had warned but Jade had too much on her mind to notice. She called on Julianne at home, taking a very big chance on whether she would let her in, but surprisingly she did. It was an emotional meeting for both of them. Julianne had found out only a few days before that her husband was conducting an affair with a woman from his office. A compromising text message had come up on Richard's phone, which resulted in Julianne confronting him about how he had used Jade to shield his perfidious behaviour.

Jade explained why she hadn't defended herself,

confessing for the first time to anyone about her severe dyslexia. Julianne was wonderfully supportive, which made Jade wonder if she should exhibit the same courage and come clean with Nic. It would be a brave step but she couldn't see how their relationship had any chance of moving forward unless he knew everything there was to know about her.

He had phoned her several times a day and each day—along with a dozen red roses—he had sent her a present. A string of pearls with matching earrings arrived first, then there was a dress from one of her favourite designers, and on the third day a bracelet encrusted with shimmering diamonds. There was a card with the bracelet but Jade could only make out his name. She ran her fingertip over and over it, wondering if he was missing her as much as he said he would. She was certainly missing him. The huge bed felt so empty at night without his long, lean limbs reaching for hers.

When Nic called soon after the bracelet arrived Jade thanked him. 'It's beautiful, Nic,' she said.

'But you shouldn't be spending so much money on me.'

'Did you get my card?' he asked.

She rolled her lips together and looked across to where she had propped it up against the latest vase of roses. 'Yes...'

'Did you read it?' he asked after a slight pause.

Jade wanted to tell him then but she couldn't bear to do it over the phone. She wanted to see his face, to make sure he wouldn't mock or ridicule her. 'I was too distracted by the diamonds,' she said in an airy tone.

There was another pause before he said, 'I will get to the hotel about six this evening. I have a meeting in the afternoon but I shouldn't be late.'

'OK,' she said. 'See you then.'

Just before Nic was due to arrive at the hotel, Jade's father called by to drop in an early birthday present. The timing couldn't have been worse, but then she had come to expect that from her father. Keith Sommerville was two drinks down and reaching for his third when Nic arrived at the penthouse.

Jade got up from the sofa and went over to greet him. 'Hi,' she said, twisting her hands in front of her awkwardly. 'My father dropped by when he heard I was in London. I hope you don't mind.'

Nic brushed his mouth against hers, once, twice and then on the third time held her mouth with his in a lingering kiss that made every cell in her body swell with longing. 'Of course I don't mind,' he said. He looked up and smiled politely at Keith. 'How are you, Mr Sommerville?'

'You'd better call me Keith now that you're my son-in-law,' he said, raising his glass of Scotch. 'Cheers.'

Nic put an arm around Jade's waist and led her back to the sofa, taking the seat beside her. It was hard to tell if the tension in her slim body was from her father's presence or his. Nic desperately hoped it wasn't his. He had spent a torturous few days missing her, aching for her each night, dreading the thought of her announcing she wanted to end their marriage. He couldn't bear the thought of spending the rest of his life without her. He was a fool for not recognising how he felt until she had gone but when had he ever recognised emotion? He had always run from it. He had done it for so long it had become automatic. He had hardly been conscious of how he compartmentalised his life until Jade had come along and unpicked the lock to his heart.

'So,' Keith said as he leaned forward to refill his glass, 'when are you two going to give me a grandchild for real? I saw that article in the press. I was looking forward to becoming a grandfather. You'd better get on with it. Jade's not getting any younger.'

Nic felt Jade cringe as she bent her head to her glass.

'All in good time, Keith,' Nic said. 'We're still on our honeymoon.'

'I hope the first one's a boy,' Keith said. 'Every man wants a son to carry on the family name and the business.'

Nic reached for Jade's hand and gave it a gentle

squeeze. 'I will be thrilled, no matter what sex any child of ours is,' he said. 'And, as to carrying on the business, that is up to our daughter if we have one. It will be her decision, not ours.'

Jade's father harrumphed and reached for his fresh Scotch and drained it. 'Well, thanks for the drink but I must love you and leave you,' he said and got to his feet.

'It was nice of you to make the time to see Jade,' Nic said, still holding Jade's stiff little hand in his.

'Well, I can't make it for her actual birthday,' he said. 'I have a golf day with my firm. But Jade doesn't mind, do you, Jade? As long as she's got her present, that's the main thing, eh?'

'Thanks for the book voucher, Dad,' Jade said in a tight voice. 'I am sure it will come in very useful.'

Nic waited until Jade's father had left their penthouse before he turned her in his arms. 'Are you OK?' he asked.

She gave him a been-there-done-that-a-million-times look. 'At least he didn't embarrass me by getting completely drunk, but I'd say he's well on his way.'

Nic frowned and brought her hand up to his chest. 'He doesn't deserve a daughter as gorgeous and talented as you.'

She looked at his shirt front rather than his eyes. 'Thank you for saying that.'

He tipped up her face. 'I mean it, *cara*. You are one of the most unique people I have ever met. I discover more and more about you every day.'

She lowered her gaze and began to fiddle with one of the buttons on his shirt. 'Nic, there's something you should know about me. Something I should have told you right from the start.'

Nic clasped both of her hands. 'I know about your reading problem,' he said.

She looked up at him in wide-eyed blinking surprise. 'You…you do?'

He nodded. 'I didn't cotton on at first. It took me a while to realise why you never responded to my text messages and never sent any of your own, and why you always asked me what I was going to order in restaurants before you made your own choice. You had already told me you never read the papers, but I couldn't work out why you were so surprised about what was written in that false report. I put it down to the fact you just hadn't had time to read it for yourself. But it wasn't until I was on my way here this evening that I finally realised why you hadn't read it.'

Jade moistened her suddenly dry mouth. 'How did you work it out?'

He smiled at her tenderly. 'You said you didn't read the card that came with the bracelet because you were distracted by the diamonds but that's not true, is it?'

She felt her cheeks heat up. 'No...'

He cupped her face in his hands. 'Do you want to know what I wrote in that card?' he asked.

She looked at him with tears shining in her eyes. 'I'm a bit frightened to ask...'

His eyes softened even further as he gazed into hers. 'I told you I loved you, that I have loved you for most of my life. I can't think of a time when I didn't love you and want to protect you. Those feelings have always been there but I have covered them up. I've done it since I was a child, I guess because I don't like being at the mercy of other people's emotions, let alone my own. It made me feel too vulnerable.'

Jade choked back a sob. 'I can't believe you love me when I'm so…so stupid.'

Nic frowned and tightened his hold on her hands. 'You are not to say that about yourself. Never, do you hear me?'

'But I caused Jon's death,' she said, struggling not to cry. 'I forgot the details of the flight. I couldn't read the itinerary my father gave me. I was so good at covering it up. I was too proud, too stubbornly proud to ask for help. I'm so ashamed…'

Nic held her close, his heart aching for all she had suffered. '*Cara*, you are not to blame your-self. It was up to the adults around you to have you properly helped and they didn't do it. I wish I had known earlier. That's why I was so surprised when you acted as if nothing had changed this afternoon when I called you. I couldn't see why you wouldn't have read the card, diamonds or no diamonds. It was only when your father was here that I finally realised. I saw the look on your face when you thanked him for the book voucher. He still doesn't have a clue, does he?'

She shook her head. 'I've always been too frightened to say anything. He puts such a high value on academic achievement. He's always at me to better myself; that's why I get book vouchers every year even though I've never read a book in my life.'

Nic held her from him to look down at her lovingly. 'That's why you've never held down a job. It's why you refuse to show your art work. It's why you married me even though you didn't want to because you so desperately needed the money, wasn't it?'

Jade had to bite the inside of her cheek to stop herself from crying. 'I feel ashamed that I only wanted to marry you for the money. I was so determined not to fall in love with you again like I did when I was sixteen. But I couldn't seem to stop myself. Everything you said, everything you did, every time you kissed or touched me made me realise how much I loved you.'

'*Tesore mio*,' he said with a catch in his voice. 'I will help you learn to read if you will help me to be a better person. I am ashamed of how shallowly I have lived my life up until now. I have sought my own goals with no thought to anyone else. Now all I can think about is you and our future. You have done that, Jade. You have changed me, just as my grandfather knew you would.'

She smiled at him as his arms wrapped securely around her. 'Do you think he suspected this might happen? That we would fall in love eventually?'

'I am sure of it,' Nic said. 'We were always bickering at family gatherings, remember? The love-hate thing is a dead giveaway.'

Jade looked at his shirt button again. 'The night of my party—I wish it had been you instead of him. I've always regretted it. You have no idea how much.'

He cupped the back of her head and held her

close against his chest. 'Do not talk of it, *cara*,' he said. 'I wish I hadn't spoken to you so harshly. Perhaps if I had been less heavy-handed in how I handled that it might never have happened. I blame myself. I should have protected you but I was too damned focused on keeping my distance in case I overstepped the mark. You were so young—so young and innocent.'

She looked up at him again. 'I feel like that young girl when I am with you,' she said. 'You make me feel as if the past hasn't happened.'

'As far as I am concerned, it hasn't,' he said, holding her close. 'It is the future we have to concentrate on now. And I think it's going to be a bright one, don't you?'

Jade smiled. 'I think it's going to be an absolutely brilliant one,' she said as his mouth came down and covered hers.

Six months later...

The exhibition was a stunning success. Every painting had a 'Sold' sticker on it and Nic was smiling from ear to ear as yet another camera aimed its lens at his beautiful pregnant wife. Jade was glowing as she had never glowed before. He could still not believe how excited he was about the prospect of becoming a father in three months' time. Each night he placed his hand on Jade's growing belly, feeling the outline of little heels and elbows that would one day be in his arms to love and protect.

Giorgio and Maya came to stand beside him. They were arm in arm, Maya's own glow another giveaway, although nothing so far had been announced in the press. 'You must be so proud of her, Nic,' Giorgio said, smiling.

'I am,' Nic said, feeling his chest swell as he looked at his gorgeous wife.

Luca and Bronte were hugging Jade in turn, making Nic feel all the more proud of how she had become such a treasured part of his family. His mother was constantly boasting of how Jade had tamed her wildest son, turning him into a devoted family man just like his older brothers.

Jade looked at him from across the gallery, her radiant smile making her green eyes dance with happiness. He went over to her and wrapped a gentle and protective arm around her expanding waist. 'You're not getting too tired being on your feet all this time, are you?' he asked.

'Not yet,' she said, snuggling in close. 'Did you see what the reviewer wrote in the exhibition pamphlet?'

He smiled indulgently. 'Why don't you read it to me, *cara*?'

Jade flicked it open and, following the words with her finger, read each one out carefully. '"Jade Sabbatini is a fresh new talent in the art world. Her stun…stun…stunning collection entitled *In Love with Rome* has drawn inter…international interest."' She grinned up at him. 'Are you proud of me, darling?'

Nic pulled her close, resting his head on the top of her silky one, the words catching in his throat as he spoke. 'Unbelievably proud, *mio piccolo*. You constantly amaze me. I am the luckiest man in the world to have you as my wife.'

Jade looped her arms around his neck, the bump of their baby joining them as one. 'I love you, Nic Sabbatini,' she said. 'I really, *really* love you.'

'You know something, *cara*?' Nic smiled as the paparazzi hustled closer to capture the moment. 'I really, *really* love you too.'

MILLS & BOON PUBLISH EIGHT LARGE PRINT TITLES A MONTH. THESE ARE THE TITLES FOR JUNE 2011.

❧

FLORA'S DEFIANCE
Lynne Graham

THE RELUCTANT DUKE
Carole Mortimer

THE WEDDING CHARADE
Melanie Milburne

THE DEVIL WEARS KOLOVSKY
Carol Marinelli

THE NANNY AND THE CEO
Rebecca Winters

FRIENDS TO FOREVER
Nikki Logan

THREE WEDDINGS AND A BABY
Fiona Harper

THE LAST SUMMER OF BEING SINGLE
Nina Harrington

MILLS & BOON PUBLISH EIGHT LARGE PRINT TITLES A MONTH. THESE ARE THE TITLES FOR JULY 2011.

❧

A STORMY SPANISH SUMMER
Penny Jordan

TAMING THE LAST ST CLAIRE
Carole Mortimer

NOT A MARRYING MAN
Miranda Lee

THE FAR SIDE OF PARADISE
Robyn Donald

THE BABY SWAP MIRACLE
Caroline Anderson

EXPECTING ROYAL TWINS!
Melissa McClone

TO DANCE WITH A PRINCE
Cara Colter

MOLLY COOPER'S DREAM DATE
Barbara Hannay